D0330211

P.O. Box 270014
Hartford, WI 53027

ISBN 0-9642304-3-7

Distributed by:
**Jews for the Preservation of
Firearms Ownership, Inc.**
P.O. Box 270143
Hartford, WI 53027
414-673-9745 — fax 414-673-9746
www.jpfo.org

Cover art by Turner Type & Design, Lacey, WA.

The Mitzvah is a work of fiction. Any resemblance between its characters and real people, living or dead is purely coincidental.

The Mitzvah by Aaron Zelman and L. Neil Smith is powerful stuff. This attention-grabbing novel tells the story of a Catholic priest forced to confront evidence that his birth parents were German Jews who hid their infant son with neighbors before being murdered in the Holocaust.

As a non-Jew, I was fascinated by the priest's efforts to investigate his birthright and understand the fundamentals of the Jewish faith. His intellectual and spiritual journey became my own.

What the priest discovers will alarm most readers. The Mitzvah clearly shows that in America, not only are many Jewish leaders and legislators ignoring the Bill of Rights, they are also ignoring the teachings of Judaism.

Like a clear diagnosis of cancer, The Mitzvah is upsetting but must not be ignored.

John Ross, author of
Unintended Consequences

One of the most important Second Amendment novels ever published. A penetrating and masterful focus on anti-gun liberals and their schizophrenic views on both firearms and self-preservation. A compelling, must-read page burner that will cause those for whom the Second Amendment is merely an embarrassment to squirm in their easy chairs.

Peter G. Kokalis,
Technical Editor
Soldier Of Fortune Magazine.

Zelman and Smith have written a book the establishment doesn't want you to read. They don't want you to get the picture that reveals just how far government has gone beyond its limits under the Constitution. Read this book. Do something the freedom-haters won't like."

Larry Pratt
Executive Director,
Gun Owners of America

Aaron Zelman and L. Neil Smith have accomplished something remarkable with The Mitzvah. It's unquestionably polemic—with the same occasional "set pieces" you'd expect in works by Ayn Rand or Robert Heinlein—but at the same time very readable. I felt I came to know the protagonist, Monsignor John Greenwood, and enjoyed spending time with him. I even woke up in the middle of the night once, thinking about John and his journey of discovery. The Mitzvah makes arguments supporting the 2nd Amendment that badly need to be made.

Andrea Millen Rich,
President
Laissez Faire Books

THE MITZVAH

For those who love freedom—
and for those who should

A Novel by
Aaron Zelman
and
L. Neil Smith

This book is gratefully dedicated to millions of men and women in the 1940s—including our own fathers, Jack Zelman, Lester Smith and Irving "Bing" Soderlund—who, confronted by fascist tyranny and butchery, accepted Patrick Henry's bargain: "Give me liberty or give me death!"

The authors take pleasure in acknowledging the assistance and encouragement provided by the following: first and foremost, our wives, Nancy Zelman and Cathy L.Z. Smith for patience above and beyond the call of duty, and Don L. Tiggre who brought us together in the first place, also Percy Bennett (Chapter Eight wouldn't have been the same without him), Dan Bylina, Tom Creasing, Adam C. Firestone, Bob Glass of Paladin Arms, Mighty Webmaster Ken Holder, Len Jackson, Pat Lilly, Dr. Carol Low, Rex F. "Baloo" May, Phil "Zathras" Murphy, James H. Neel, Eleanor Owen, Roger L. Owen, Andrea Millen Rich, J. Neil Schulman, David Segal, Roger L. Smith, Richard W. Stevens, Vin Suprynowicz, John Taylor, Katherine von Tour, Eric Western, and especially Rabbi Reuven Mermelstein and Dr. Sarah Thompson for their invaluable contributions to Chapters Eleven and Twelve. The phrase "The Machinery of Freedom" in Chapter Sixteen is, of course, the title of David Friedman's classic work on individual liberty.

All rights reserved. Copyright ©1999 by Aaron Zelman and L. Neil Smith. No part of this book may be reproduced or transmitted in any form or by any other means, electronic or mechanical, including photocopying, recording, or by any information storage or retrieval system, without written permission from the authors, except for the inclusion of brief quotations in a review.

Printed in the United States of America.

TABLE OF CONTENTS

If someone comes to kill you,
arise quickly and kill him.
— The Talmud

CHAPTER ONE:
JOHN GREENWOOD

Suddenly there was another hand on the car door handle.

John looked up, directly into a hard-driving sleet that stung like needles, into the mild eyes, crinkled at their corners with a kind of cosmically patient amusement, of a very old man—a rather tall and gangly old man—whose gaze met John's at a level almost equal to his own.

"Well, my boy," the old man's accent was vaguely European, and he seemed to chuckle as he spoke. "Are we going to stand here until we freeze solid in our places, or are we going to get into this nice warm taxi?"

It was the first time in a long while—he was 55—that anyone had called John "my boy". Whistling jet engines overhead, dense crowds of passengers ramming themselves in and out of automatic doors (mostly with their eyes squeezed tightly against the storm), a certain tang of kerosene in the air, and a midwinter storm that would have paralyzed any other city for days. He'd have known where he was even with his own eyes closed. There wasn't any other place in the world quite like O'Hare International Airport, just as there wasn't any other city like Chicago.

Sleet-storm or not, he was glad to be home.

"Well?"

Somewhere, a public address system was explaining who could park in the white zone and who couldn't. John imagined he could feel the cold and dampness of the half-melted gray slush around his feet begin to creep into the sole-seams of his shoes. The fact was, he was wearing rubber outers which prevented that. Nevertheless he pressed the chrome-plated button with his right thumb and pulled the handle, having to open the door with a wrenching motion to break the gasketing of ice that held it shut.

A blast of steamy-hot air smelling of—what, stale cheeseburger and French fries?—enveloped them both as he helped the old man into the cab along with the small case that was all he seemed to be carrying. It wasn't a briefcase like John's, but something unfamiliar in size and proportion, perhaps a bit like a small vanity case.

John wrestled his own heavily-topcoated bulk into the cab and onto the seat beside the old man, reflecting—not for the first time—that it wasn't always a good thing to be a large, powerful man. More often than not, it seemed to be a disadvantage in a world built, for the most part, for smaller people. He was only six feet two, weighed 220 pounds, but since adolescence, he'd never had a bed that truly fit him.

"Would one of y'gentlemen be after kindly closin' the bloody door? 'Tis that cold out there!" The cabbie flipped the flag on his meter, almost shouting over the noise of the cab's heater fan. "I thank you. An' where might y'be after goin' on this fine, miserable mornin', gents?"

"St. Gabriel's rectory," John answered.

At the same moment the old man said, "Piper Arms Hotel—why that's—"

"Just across the street from the rectory," John finished for him, more than a little startled. "Daley Street, between Champagne and Urbana."

"That it is, Father Greenwood," the cabby nodded his approval over his gloved hands on the steering wheel. "Or should I be after sayin' Monsignor?"

"You know me?" John was beginning not to like this. Another wild coincidence would be too much. "I don't believe you're one of my parisioners."

"An' more's the pity it is, too, yer Worship. I saw y'on TV just last week—Channel Nine it was—tellin' 'em all about Catholic Youth hockey." He pronounced "Catholic" and "youth" as if there were no H in either word. John thought he was hearing the accent of Northern Ireland—Belfast or something. "An' that sad it made me not t'have a fine son o'me own t'be coached by such a fine coach as yerself."

John nodded politely, not quite sure what to make of his newfound—and he had no doubt extremely transitory—fame. "Why, thank you, er ... "

"Billy. Billy McCarthy." No H in "McCarthy", either. He was young, perhaps no more than 30, with two days' beard and a lurid scar stretching under his greasy ballcap from his temple to just above his ear.

He'd twisted around in his seat and gave both men a grin. "An' it's sorry I am not t'shake the hand of ya." He knocked on the thick plexiglass separating his half of the cab from theirs, his voice coming to them around its top and sides. "This thing went up the day after I got me head bashed for fifty-seven dollars an' thirty-three cents."

"Tirty-tree cents," he'd said. "Pity it didn't go up the day before."

"Pity, indeed," John replied, almost pulled by the moment into parroting Billy's lilting accent. He saw the old man shake his head, with what—amusement? In the momentary silence, the wipers up front slapped back and forth vainly across the streaming windshield as the heater roared. John pointedly shoved the sleeves of his topcoat, jacket, and shirt up his wrist to expose his watch. "Shouldn't we be getting on? The meter's running."

"Aye, that we should, yer Worship." McCarthy gave the wheel a heave as he floored the gas pedal. "An' I'll make up the time t'be sure!"

The cab cut into the heavy concourse traffic, pushing both men deep into the backseat cushions. John felt a little prayer to St. Christopher form on his lips as they surged past other vehicles—wallowing through the slush like so many prehistoric animals in a tar-pit—accompanied by the honking horn and cheerful Gaelic curses of their driver.

CHAPTER TWO:
ALBERT MENDELSOHN

It was he!

Before they'd gone a mile—the cab sending up twin rooster tails of semiliquid snow behind them—McCarthy had jammed a cassette into the player on his dashboard and was rewarded with Chuck Berry singing "Memphis". He glanced back at his passengers—narrowly missing the sooty back end of a city bus in the process—and turned the volume down.

Albert found himself wishing he'd left the volume high. Anything to prevent a tremor in his voice from betraying him. Could there be two like that in the world—that mushroom-shaped birthmark he'd seen on the priest's wrist when he'd shoved his sleeve up to look at his watch?

It was he!

"John Greenwood," said the younger man, thrusting out a hand, unaware of the turmoil in his fellow passenger's mind. "I'm monsignor of the Church of St. Gabriel Possenti of Isola, and, as our friend up front says, part-time hockey coach. I'm just home from a conference in Denver."

"Catholic Youth Hockey." The older man nodded, doing his best to smile back without revealing his racing heart. At 75 years of age, between a world war and the exigencies of business, he'd had some practice. He scrutinized John closely, as if to

9

convince himself of something. How long had it been since the last time he'd seen that birthmark?

"Catholic Youth Athletics," Greenwood corrected. "A more general organizational agenda than Mr. McCarthy may have given you to believe. As for hockey it's ... well, you might say it's a special calling of mine."

Somewhat dazed, the old man nodded again and at last reached for the monsignor's hand which he found warm, strong, and surprisingly calloused to the touch. A man, then, who worked hard at what he did. "I am Albert Mendelsohn, Monsignor, of Schoten, near Antwerp, in Belgium. I am a merchant, calling upon some of my commercial accounts in Chicago. And a good thing, too, since that is where we seem to be going."

The younger man chuckled politely at Albert's joke, not realizing the character it had required to make it. He released the old man's hand and settled back in the seat. "A merchant in what, if I may ask?"

Albert shrugged. "You may ask: *diamenten*—diamonds," He watched John's eyes go immediately to the case he held on his lap. People were always the same, even this one. "No, I do not bring them. They come by Federal Express, once they have been ordered and paid for. "

The monsignor nodded, expressing approval of the arrangement. "May I ask you why, at an age when many other men would long since have retired, you continue to call on your commercial accounts, here, or anywhere else? I don't mean to be nosy—not very nosy anyway—I just sense the makings of a good sermon here, about not giving in to age."

Albert grinned, and this time it was genuine and unforced. "Tell your parishioners it is for the same reason that a man of your age—who should be at least *thinking* about a rocking chair, shawl, pipe, and slippers—continues to pursue such a dangerous sport, dashing about on a sheet of ice with knives strapped to your feet and a club in your hands. I think because you cannot imagine doing anything else."

John laughed, and the open, hearty sound of it had much to tell the older man sitting beside him. "I'm afraid you have me there, Mr. Mendelsohn—"

"Albert. Call me Albert. I like this American custom of first names."

"Very well, Albert, then you must call me John. And you're right, of course. It's ironic—sleet and slush at the airport ... "He carefully lowered his voice: "A harrowing drive through more sleet and slush—a typical Lake Michigan winter storm—then even more sleet and slush at my own doorstep. Yet I want nothing more than to get onto the ice of my home rink again, and give my valiant young warriors an exhaustive workout. That, Mr. Mendelsohn is my ideal: practice creating perfection."

"Ah?" Albert found that he liked listening to this younger man talk.

"The air inside the rink, Albert, is cool, calm, dry, and clean—especially since I personally sabotaged the radiant heaters over the bleachers which, when they're on, make the entire place smell like the inside of a well-used running shoe. Delicate sinuses, I guess. I'm also the only coach I know of who makes his team launder their jerseys between outings. You can't begin to imagine what the average team smells like at the beginning of practice, or a game, let alone at the end."

"I will try to remember—or forget, I am unsure which. Now tell me ... "

Albert engaged the monsignor in small talk, mostly about hockey, a game about which he knew absolutely nothing and wanted to know less, until—

"Piper Arms Hotel, gents," McCarthy cried cheerfully. "We're here!"

The cab half slid to a stop before an old, worn, comfortable-looking building. Across the street through the diminishing storm, Albert could make out the gray Gothic arches of a vaguely church-like building, flanked on either side by newer looking red brick annexes. McCarthy announced the fare and before Albert could move, leaped from the cab, jerked the rear door open, and reached in for the old man's bag.

"I thought you drivers didn't do this any more," Albert informed him, manipulating bills which, while familiar, were still foreign and awkward. It was difficult getting the right ones without losing them all to the eternal Chicago wind.

McCarthy grinned. "To the Devil with security. 'Preferred treatment for preferred customers', I always say." He winked broadly at Greenwood.

"Moreover, any friend of the monsignor's is a friend of mine."

He took the money and, as he reached in again to help Albert out of the cab, the old man caught an unmistakable glimpse—blackened, polished steel sandwiched between two smooth hardwood panels—of a small revolver dangling under McCarthy's left armpit between his rough, heavy, turtleneck sweater and his short, sweat-stained leather jacket.

McCarthy winked again, this time at Albert, now standing with him beside the cab. "An' better t'be tried by twelve than carried by six."

"Even so," the old man advised him. It never failed to give him a warm, comfortable feeling, being reminded that there were decent and productive individuals who went about armed, as well as the thugs, uniformed and otherwise. "It never hurts to be careful about what people can see. A fellow like you has two sets of enemies, you know, those who would rob or kill him, and those who would punish him for attempting to prevent it."

McCarthy laughed and pointed in at the laminated copy of his cab-driver's license, diplayed on the visor for all to see, a reminder that there was nothing even remotely resembling a free economy on the shores of Lake Michigan. "D'you think I'm all that likely t'forget it?" Then he nodded. "Nonetheless, I'll remember what y'said."

"And I," replied Albert, "will ask for you the next time I need a taxi."

CHAPTER THREE:
ELEANOR DURYEA

Having dropped Albert off at the comfortable old Piper Arms, a building John had never much noticed or given a thought to in all the years he'd been at St. Gabriel's, McCarthy pulled an illegal U-turn in the middle of the block and braked the cab in front of the rectory.

Angered and depressed by what he, too, had seen under the cabbie's armpit as Albert had climbed out—what was the world coming to, when a man felt he had to go armed and ready to kill his fellow man just to make a living?—he paid McCarthy without conversation, took his briefcase, and trudged through the salted, half-frozen slush that had gathered on the sidewalk, toward the rectory, set well back from the street, where he maintained his residence and office.

"Monsignor Greenwood!" Eleanor Duryea looked up from her desk as he came in the door, having done his best to stamp the slush off. He closed it behind him, as always annoyed at the rattling venetian blind that covered the long glass portion of its surface. Eleanor looked delighted to see him; that helped a bit to dispel the gloom that had settled over him at the end of the cab ride. "Welcome home!"

Eleanor was a plump, dark-haired woman pushing 60 from one side or another. Her hair, nails, and upswept eyeglasses came straight from a previous generation. She admitted to having lost— and regained—at least 3000 pounds over the past 30 years, sometimes referring to herself as a "Weight Watcher's dropout". Her dark eyes sparkled with quick intelligence and a sense of humor; she never failed to remind John of the little old ladies in *Arsenic and Old Lace*.

A long-time parish member whose children were grown up, she'd begun work here some years ago as a volunteer when her husband had died. Now, for better or worse, the church had become the center of her life. John had more or less created a job for her and never regretted it. For one thing, she was highly competent with computers. It was quite a sight, watching her pudgy little fingers race across a keyboard or steer a mouse. He had learned—by trial and many errors—to write his own letters with a word processor, but he was glad he had Eleanor to fix things went they went wrong.

"It's good to be back, Eleanor." John set his briefcase on a chair beside the door (the place served as a waiting room as well as Eleanor's office), removed his topcoat and scarf and hung them on a rack, then stooped to pull the rubber covers off his favorite pair of shoes, a classic pair of Allen Edmonds wingtips which he considered his only extravagance. The cumbersome rubber objects always made him think of his mother, who had never let him leave home without them in the winter.

"You want it now," she asked, holding up the notebook she used to keep track of his messages and appointments. Eleanor was more than his secretary or he'd never have been able to afford her. She also did administrative chores for this and three other churches in nearby neighborhoods. "Or would you care for a nice hot cup of tea, first?"

"Coffee, I think—don't get up, I'll get it." He ran a hand through his thick, graying hair. "It's been a long day already and it's only—11 o'clock? My watch is still on Mountain time."

He went to the cabinet, crowded two packages of coffee, as usual, into the basket instead of one, then took the carafe to a small half bath where he rinsed and filled it. He'd been promising Eleanor to find the money for a faucet filter—windy city water was terrible, especially after a trip to the Rockies— but kept forgetting until moments like this. He returned to pour the water into the top of the machine, setting the glass vessel on the warmer. In a moment it began to refill with rich, hot, dark brown liquid. The room started to have that wonderful aroma he associated with getting down to work.

Eleanor kept a tiny refrigerator in the corner behind her desk, just the size to serve as a stand for the fax machine. From it she took a carton of half-and-half and handed it to John who spooned a considerable amount of Nestle Quik into his cup before filling it with coffee. He thought of this as his only vice. Stirring cream into the mixture, he returned the carton to the refrigerator, then led Eleanor into his office where he sat down.

Not a bad room, he thought. Four walls painted

a neutral beige, one with a door to the anteroom. The one thing he really disliked was the long, narrow window in the fourth wall, behind him, way up at the ceiling, Frank Lloyd Wright-style. It was impossible to build an air conditioner into, and it let a cold draft fall on his neck. The pigeons, apparently, found it a comfortable place to roost. He had two big old-fashioned glass-fronted bookcases, full of books, a couple of garish yellow upholstered chairs for guests, a leather couch from Goodwill, and a small table piled with books he couldn't get into the bookcases. His parents had given him an expensive Persian rug that made the place feel warm and homey.

Atop the bookcases stood more than a dozen hockey trophies. Here and there around the walls were framed photographs of the many youth teams he'd coached over the years. On a stand near the door rested a taped and battered glove which had once belonged to the Montreal Canadians' Maurice "Rocket" Richard, his boyhood idol. These days he was a Patrick Roy fan.

His desk was large and plain, made of oak. Burnt-in markings inside the drawers indicated that in World War II, it had belonged to an Army hospital in Texas. He tried to keep its surface un-cluttered. At present it held his telephone, a lamp with a turned wooden base that had been another gift, a small stack of papers, and half a dozen hockey pucks he used as paperweights and to hold books open to the right page when he was copying from them for sermons and other purposes.

"Okay," he told her, taking a deep, appreciative drink of his coffee as she sat down in a chair facing the desk, "whatcha got?"

Eleanor flipped back the cover of her steno book. "Bishop Camelle's office called earlier this morning to say there'll be an organizational meeting tomorrow regarding United Nations Appreciation Week."

John nodded. This was a separate thing—a Chicago thing—from UN Day, October 24. This wouldn't happen until March, three months from now, and would require lots of effort and coordination. As an antiwar activist in his youth and a lifelong advocate of world peace, he looked forward to it. He glanced up at the pictures on the wall of Dorothy Day, the grand old lady of Catholic pacifism, and Thomas Merton, whom he regarded as his intellectual forebears. (Eleanor had a photo of Mother Theresa on the wall behind her desk and one of Ghandi across the room.) He was tempted to put up pictures of the Berrigan brothers, but thought that might be going a bit far.

As a "child of the 60s", John had been influenced by philosophers and theologians like Soren Kierkegaard, Dietrich Bonhoeffer, Paul Tillich, Karl Jaspers, even Jean-Paul Sartre. He had photos of some of them in his private rooms. Pragmatically, he remained a devotee of Day, who had been editor and publisher of *The Catholic Worker*, of Merton, and an admirer of the Berrigans. He was agnostic—less unusual among priests than might be imagined—concerned more with social justice than traditional

Church teachings, an advocate of quasi-Marxist "liberation theology", and a devout pacifist.

"Monsignor?"

"Sorry, Eleanor." He sat up a little straighter and took another drink of coffee. "Got lost in my thoughts. Please go on."

Eleanor nodded, accustomed to his ways. "The bishop's secretary said you're supposed to bring your best and brightest ideas with you. The diocese wants to make a real show of it this first year. The Japanese ambassador will be the mayor's guest of honor."

Inwardly gratified that he'd been called on by Camelle—a man notoriously hard to please—what he said was, "Ambassador or not, I hope this meeting doesn't drag on. I've got an important hockey practice tomorrow evening."

Eleanor nodded again, unsurprised. "That Mrs. Gibbs called three times while you were gone." There was disapproval in her voice. "Honestly, for someone who isn't even a member of this parish ..."

He tried not to grin as her words trailed off. Sheila Hensley Gibbs had been his high school sweetheart, class of 1959. She'd only been half joking in 1960 when he'd entered the seminary and she'd accused him of jilting her for the church. Over the ensuing decades, she'd called him every year or so. He'd found it mildly embarrassing, but tolerated it. Lately, for about the past four months, she'd been calling him more frequently, even threatening to take him out to dinner. Eleanor was scandalized and quite incapable of concealing it.

"Your mother called day before yesterday and Dr. Sinclair called yesterday. Both of them said they'd call back. Your mother wanted to make sure you'd taken your asthma inhaler to the 'Mile High City'."

He chuckled. He hadn't needed an inhaler for 30 years, thanks to the brisk exercise in clean, cool air he got nearly every day. He'd explained that to his mother a thousand times but either she didn't believe him or she didn't remember. Dr. Thornton Sinclair—"Kitch"—was his oldest and best friend. They'd been college roomates.

"I'll phone my mother back this afternoon, although I spoke to her from Denver, and return Mrs. Gibbs' call—please don't look at me that way, Eleanor, she's married and so am I, in a manner of speaking. I'll give Kitch a call, too. Past time we had lunch."

"Monsignor," Eleanor closed her notebook and rested it on her lap. "Father Joseph seems very upset about a couple of his young soccer players getting hurt. He said he'd be in the gymnasium doing inventory and maintenance. Should I call him?"

"No," he shook his head, "I'll go to him. Keep the home fires burning—and in case I decide to accept that dinner invitation from Mrs. Gibbs, you might polish up my chastity belt."

"Monsignor!" Her eyes went wide, then she realized he was joking, giggled quietly, and went back to her desk.

CHAPTER FOUR: FATHER JOSEPH SPAGELLI

Like John, Father Joseph Spagelli was enthusiastically active in church athletic programs, although—being a man of the 90s, as he sometimes put it jokingly to the monsignor—he coached soccer teams. The older priest had always preferred hockey and would refer on such occasions to the younger priest's selection as "baby kickyball".

The rectory at St. Gabriel's occupied the left wing of an annex built a century after the church itself, one that wrapped around the older building on three sides, left, right, and rear. The right wing consisted of a high school-sized gymnasium and related facilities which the monsignor reached by walking through the chancel of the church. The rear part of the annex was used primarily for storage and was not only difficult and dusty to wend one's way through, but was probably in violation of city and county fire codes.

John spied Father Joseph, clipboard in one hand, pencil in the other, ostensibly inspecting a tall wire rack that held basketballs and other athletic equipment.

What spoiled the impression that he was working hard on the inventory was that, from the moment John entered the vast cavelike room, all through his long trek around the sacred hardwood to the far side of the building—as he walked, his shoes made little sqeaking sounds on the floor that they never seemed to make anywhere else; they reminded him of bat noises—he didn't see Father Joseph move a muscle. The young man stood staring at the letters SPALDING on a ball as if they were Babylonian cuneiform and meaningless to him—and yet somehow vitally important.

"Joseph?" Inhaling the unmistakably athletic odors of leather, canvas, rubber, and generations of human sweat, the monsignor opened the cage door; its hinges shrieked embarrassingly and echoed though the gym. Still the young priest didn't move.

"Father Joseph!" John stood beside him now. Spagelli flinched, then slowly unwound, turning to his superior. He wore faded jeans and a clean but badly-worn Catholic Youth Athletics sweatshirt. A nickel-plated whistle hung on a dirty cord around his neck. He was somewhat slight of stature and darkly complected, with a Mediterranean nose that reminded John of Al Pacino's. At the moment his eyes were red-rimmed as if he'd been crying. His black, beatnik-style moustache and goatee were normally trimmed with a precision that might have been deemed a sign of sinful pride by a stricter standard than John maintained. But today his hair was uncombed and he hadn't shaved since at least yesterday.

"Monsignor. Sorry. I'm ... preoccupied, I guess." He glanced at the clipboard as if surprised to find it in his hand, appearing to find no more meaning in it than he had in the basketball lettering. He slid his pencil behind the clip, set them on a cabinet, and sighed.

"Anything I can do for you, boss?"

John laid a hand on his shoulder. "Eleanor told me you wanted to see me. Concerning a couple of your soccer players?"

"That was it, all right," Spagelli replied. "Could we step outside a moment, Monsignor? I need to clear my head."

John knew exactly what that meant, but didn't mind. He followed Spagelli through the rear door of the building, out into a little concrete courtyard meant to hold a dumpster. By accident, it also captured the early afternoon light and was the warmest, calmest spot on the church grounds. The storm had begun to clear off and the sky was almost blue. *Welcome home, John*, the monsignor thought. For some reason his next passing thought was of Sheila Gibbs.

Spagelli fished around in his left hip pocket, extracting a badly crushed pack of Marlboros from which he took a bent and flattened cigarette. From his right front pocket, he pulled a Bic lighter. With the cigarette in his mouth and hands cupped around the lighter, he thumbed the wheel, puffed the cigarette alight, put the lighter away, repocketed the pack, and took a deep draw of smoke.

"Better," he told John, looking him in the eye for the first time. "Much better. Hard to think without a cigarette in my hand."

John had quit smoking five years ago, but even now, the whiff of tobacco smoke with its thin, acrid overtone of nicotine, inspired a moment's craving. He shook his head, "Maybe it should have been vows of chastity, poverty, and abstinence from the vile weed."

Spagelli laughed dutifully, then his face was serious again. "Two of my kids are shot, Monsignor!" The young priest was beside himself with rage and pain; his voice quavered as he spoke. "Remember my big midfielder, Julio Apodaca?"

John didn't, but he nodded encouragingly.

"He was wounded last night and caught carrying a pistol after some kind of gang fight. I talked to him and his mother at the emergency room. He was taken straight from there to the prison ward. Once he's well enough, they'll take him to Cook County. Even though he was strapped to a gurney, they had him in handcuffs, leg-irons, and belly-chains. Monsignor, I never saw anything like it."

He took a long, hard drag on his cigarette, held and released it, then flicked the ashes off onto the concrete where he ground them underfoot before an eddy of wind could carry them away. Settling against the warmest wall, he slid down until he was squatting at its base. John stood with his arms crossed, watching him. It was really too cold to be out here, he thought, but Joseph needed him.

"The other one, Jorge Velazquez, had just died in the same emergency room, virtually in my arms!" John could see he was near tears again. "Jorge wasn't a gang kid. He took second place in his high school science fair last month! He just happened to be in the wrong place at the wrong time, taking his sister to a movie!"

"Did ... what was his name, Julio, shoot him?"

"No, no," Spagelli shook his head. "Julio had a nine millimeter. Jorge was killed with a shotgun. His sister was hit, too, by the same blast, but not badly. They taped her ankles up and I took her home. There wasn't anything more to do at the hospital!"

John pulled the collar of his jacket up around his ears, although it did him little good. The sun was shining, but the damp wind was testing his resolve. Or maybe it was the conversation that he found suddenly chilling. Sitting on his haunches with his back against the sun-warmed wall, Father Joseph didn't seem to feel it.

"Thing is, Monsignor, I work with these kids every day, I think I'm getting to know them, sometimes I even think I'm helping them to see some kind of future beyond the hellholes like Cabrini Green. Then something like this happens, and all of a sudden I realize I'm not making the least bit of difference."

"How many kids do you coach, Joseph, a couple hundred all told?" Soccer was a less expensive sport to support than hockey and the program could field a great many more players.

The young priest took another draw on his cigarette and nodded.

"Something like that, Monsignor. More in the summertime, of course."

"And two—that's one percent—get hurt. And one of those two was completely innocent.

Wouldn't you say that's a pretty fair—"

"No I wouldn't, Monsignor! These kids aren't numbers! They aren't percentages on a wall chart! They're real live, unique, absolutely irreplaceable human beings! Half the people who ever lived are alive today. Out of the whole 10 or 11 billion, nobody in history was ever quite like Jorge Velazquez, nowhere on the whole planet, and nobody ever will be again! All because ... because ... " He stood up, threw his cigarette down, and stamped it savagely.

John unfolded his arms and put his hands in his pockets. He expected to hear what he'd said himself so many times about the easy availability of guns. But it was important to listen: "Because?"

"Because ... " Father Joseph took his eyes off the concrete at his feet and looked up thoughtfully at John. "Because we teach them to read and write—and play soccer and hockey—but we never teach them to take care of themselves. *Really* take care of themselves."

He returned to the rectory having done his poor best, he thought, to counsel the distraught young priest. Joseph was entertaining strange ideas, among them, severe doubts about his vocation. John had suffered similar doubts over the years and had eventually worked his way though them— often with Kitch Sinclair's help. Beyond that, there hadn't been much he could say. Perhaps he was tired from his morning travels. Could a person suffer jet lag just flying from one time zone to the next?

With that, a cheerful thought occurred to him. He hadn't known for certain when he would return to Chicago from Denver, so he hadn't made any appointments for today. There happened to be a splendid old leather couch in his office, rather like those proverbially used by psychiatrists. With his door closed and Eleanor to guard it for him, he could probably sneak in a therapeutic little nap before lunch.

As he took his Allen Edmonds off and lay down, he couldn't help thinking about Father Joseph. Half-consciously, he reflected on his own life—and on the recurring nightmare that had ultimately led him to his calling.

In the dream, John always saw himself ...

Saw himself ...

Saw himself ...

"Mommy! Daddy!" He was a small, terrified child, lost amidst a moving forest of gigantic legs in the crushing mass of an hysterical mob. Hoarsely shouting men scrambled past nearly trampling him, women screamed, and, incongruously, he heard the pop-pop-pop *of fireworks, growing louder and louder until the noise became the very universe itself.*

Suddenly, from a nearby doorway, there emanated a blinding white light which no one but John seemed to notice. From within the brilliance a huge, man-sized cross could be seen in silhouette. It grew sharper and more distinct until John could see that it wasn't a cross at all, but the figure of a kindly-faced, bearded man standing tall with his arms spread wide, stretched out to receive him.

The open arms of Jesus Christ himself were being

extended to receive him ...

CHAPTER FIVE:
RACHEL AND RUVEN

At long last, Albert found himself alone in his usual room at the Piper Arms.

It had been a difficult 20 minutes for the old man, from taxi to desk clerk, from desk clerk to bellhop, and from bellhop to blessed solitude. Ralph Waldo Emerson Sykes, the desk clerk, either hadn't noticed Albert all but tap-dancing with excitement on the customer's side of the counter, or had been too well-mannered to mention it. Albert had known Waldo since he was a little boy playing around the Piper Arms then being managed by his father. He'd even contributed a little to get the boy through hotel management school.

The bellhop—new to Albert—had received a bridegroom's tip, an unusually large gratuity, simply for vanishing promptly.

Albert tossed his case on the bed. He hadn't let the bellhop carry it. Although there was nothing of value in it, its predecessors had had a way of disappearing once it was known what he did for a living. And he was very well known here. The case was followed by his scarf, hat, and the heavy old tweed topcoat he shrugged out of hastily before almost diving for the bedside telephone. The number he punched into it was long but extremely familiar, and before the less modern instrument at the other end had rung more than three times, it was answered by a voice he knew better than any other in the world.

"*'Allo?*"

"Rachel!"

He couldn't keep himself from yelling into the mouthpiece, in part because he was beside himself over the morning's strange and wonderful events, in part because of a lifetime of experience (now obsolete) with long distance calls. His brother Ruven, more technologically sophisticated than he, had explained communications satellites to him, but it hadn't altered the way Albert had with a telephone.

"*Albert?*"

Rachel's pronunciation of his name was different than that of the Americans he'd just left. Nor was the language she used that of the country to which he'd placed his call. It was unusual for him to phone this soon after arrival. "*Was ist los mit dir?*"

He replied to his wife in the same German she had used: "Rachel, nothing's wrong. I believe that I have found him! Send the documents—and call Ruven in Johannesburg!"

He was answered by a long silence at Rachel's end. Albert knew she was struggling with her own measure of astonishment, confusion, and disbelief. Then: "You have found *him*, Etta's boy? My God, after all these years? How—no, no, never mind that now. Do you have any idea what time it is in Johannesburg? Or here?"

"Yes, I know." Albert couldn't help smiling. She'd have asked that if it were high noon, which it would be here in an hour. He saw her in his mind's eye, standing beside the stairs in the dimly-lit hall of their narrow, three-story house, the heavy black handpiece of the receiver held to her face. Her hair was dark, as it had been the first time they met. It had never faded from its natural brown and made her look 20 years younger than her threescore and twelve. In Schoten it would be six o'clock in the late, gloomy afternoon. Cold, no doubt raining. He often wondered why they lived there.

In Johannesburg where Ruven attended to the buying end of their business, it had no doubt been another of those damnably bright, summer-in-December days, and it was seven o'clock in the evening. If it had been Ruven on the phone, he would have accused his brother of wearing Bermuda shorts, basking in the sun, and drinking daquiris or whatever they drank in South Africa. It was an old joke between them.

He and Rachel spoke of details: where he'd stored the documents; the combination of the safe (which she knew better than he did); what folders to look in. None of it was really necessary. Each was simply unwilling to let go of the other on the telephone. This was a day they'd believed would never arrive. More than that, half a century and he loved her more than the day they had married.

Reluctantly finishing his conversation with his wife, he hung his coat neatly with his hat and scarf in the little closet area the hotel provided, and placed his travelling case under the nightstand, having removed an alarm clock, toothbrush, and comb. He turned on the TV, punching numbers for CNN Headline News into the remote and turning the volume all the way down. Half of what they said was lies, anyway, and the other half was evidence that they weren't very bright. But it was movement and color and kept him company a long way from home.

Tomorrow had already promised to be busy. Now doubly so: he had to rearrange things so he could go and see that priest again, once the papers arrived. If he knew Rachel, and he ought to, they were on the way already. He suspected his brother was booking a flight to Chicago this very minute, having cancelled the trip to Moscow he'd planned to make. Albert had only one business appointment scheduled for this afternoon. He would use the time before and after getting as much rest as he could. If he could.

Lifting the receiver again, he pushed buttons for room service and ordered lunch. Then he removed his tie, took his jacket and vest and draped them carefully over a chair, then finally removed his shoes. He stretched out on the bed waiting for his food, taking in the not-unpleasant smells of slightly yellowing wallpaper, aromatic bath soap, freshly-laundered bedclothes, clean towels, and whatever solvent they used to keep the carpet clean.

Albert loved hotels. Idly, he recalled the last time he'd seen "John Greenwood", a nightmarish scene in their native Frankfurt two and a half lifetimes ago as these things are reckoned, where hundreds of helpless men, women, and children were being rounded up by uniformed thugs—it was generally believed for transportation to the Nazi concentration camps.

Albert and his brother Ruven had watched in hiding from a secret basement chamber. They were being helped to elude the roundup by the White Rose Society, a group of German Christians—most of them very young people—who opposed the Nazis. Although Albert assumed there must have been survivors somewhere, every one of the society's members he'd personally known had been murdered by the Nazis, their young heads sheared off by a clean, efficient, modern hydraulic guillotine.

Albert and Ruven had eventually become partisans, and—His reveries were interrupted by a knock on the door, room service bringing him his midday meal. He arose from the bed to answer the door and let the young woman bring the tray in and place it on the table by the window. He handed her a tip—not so generous as the one he'd given the bellboy—and saw her out.

American food.

Albert had always loved American food, considering it the only weakness he would willingly give in to. He always looked forward to it as a high point of his trip here. Nothing fancy. To him, everyday American food had the virtues of simplicity—almost honesty, one might say—and straightforwardness. Nor was it always overcooked or greasy like the food back home could be. There were many things he loved about Rachel. Her cooking wasn't one of them. (Except for her strudel, over which, he often imagined, great battles might have been fought in classical times, as had been over the mere physical beauty of Helen of Troy. He had never said this to Rachel, however, fearing she might not take it as he meant it.)

From time to time, someone he went to lunch with asked if he were Orthodox, Conservative, or Reform, seeing the kinds of things he let himself eat. The answer that sprang to mind—although not always to his lips—was that he was a *partisan*. He had spent the first part of his adult life eating whatever came to hand, often on the run. On two occasions he'd eaten snails, once in the cellar of a famous French restaurant, the other in the depths of a gloomy forest, swarming with Nazis. He doubted there was another as religiously devout as he, but ritual practices regarding food had been too expensive a conceit in the war against Hitler. Rachel kept kosher at home. That was fine and he cooperated. When he was away from home, he kept *partisan*.

This afternoon it was a double cheeseburger and French fries, with a Coca-Cola *and* a thick chocolate milk shake. He planned to walk to his first and only appointment of the day, and didn't worry that the meal would lay heavily on his stomach. He'd been thinking about it during the whole long journey here—before he'd seen that birthmark on Greenwood's wrist—and hadn't touched the dreadful substances on plastic dishes they'd threatened him with on the airplane. Frankly he expected better from first class seating. So much for that assumption—assumptions being the mother of all major disappointments.

Not long after the girl departed, there was another knock on the door. When he opened it, he saw Ralph Sykes standing before him with a long, wide metal box in his hands. In his excitement, Albert had almost forgotten about this, althought it was a ritual he went through in every hotel in every city where he did business.

"Mr. Waldbrunn said you'd be wanting this, sir,"

"Indeed, Ralph, thank you." It was a safe deposit box, kept for him by the owner and general manager of the Piper Arms, an old partisan friend Willi Waldbrunn, who must be very busy not to bring it himself. Perhaps he was breaking Ralph in on the more subtle aspects of the trade. Albert took it, found some money in his pocket and gave it to the clerk, who nodded, smiled, turned on his heel and headed back to the elevator. Albert closed the door, threw the deadbolt and fastened the chain, then took the metal box to the table, found the right key on his keychain (he had a drawer full of them at home, all carefully labelled), and opened the box.

Inside, a thick stack of 20 dollar bills—emergency money—lay beside an Uncle Mike's black nylon belt slide holster and pouch which held a Dan Wesson .357 magnum and three "speed loaders" filled with Winchester Silvertip hollowpoints. Eighteen rounds, Albert thought, a lucky number—

to life!. And while it was true that a semiautomatic pistol was more efficient, a revolver didn't leave tell-tale casings behind for the FBI and its "Star-Fire" system to identify. There were a couple of spare barrels for it—the Dan Wesson was unique in this respect—so that, once used for self-defense, the old barrel, with its giveaway markings, could be discarded. One thing he'd learned in the war that he'd *never* forget: *never* let yourself be disarmed by law, decree, edict, or local custom.

How many *armed* Jews had been marched into the gas chambers?

Answer: none.

Gratified to be armed again, Albert spent less time savoring his long anticipated meal than he might have, had things gone differently this morning, and more wrestling with the moral dilemma he now saw facing him. He'd been happy beyond measure to discover what was certain to be the child he'd lost track of in Frankfurt, and so had Rachel. Ruven would be, as well.

"But have I the right—" he asked aloud, as he often did when reasoning as hard as he could. (He picked up a sliver of dill pickle and put it in his mouth.) "—can there *be* such a thing as a right to upset this John Greenwood's life? Possibly even his whole future?"

He shook his head and took a long, hard, soothing pull on the milkshake. Somewhere he'd heard that chocolate contains chemicals that stimulate the brain. True or false, the idea was certainly attractive, and just now he needed all the help he could get.

"Think! Think!" he demanded of himself. "Remember the promise we made, Ruven and I! There was nothing we could do to stop the bastards from dragging Etta and her David off and murdering them."

Suddenly he was aware of his reflection in the mirror on the back of the bathroom door, an old man sitting on the edge of the bed—he hadn't noticed that he'd gotten up from the table and sat down again—head bowed over his lap and fists clenched impotently at his sides.

"Nothing!" he repeated, as if pleading with his reflection. He raised his right hand, fist clenched, and shook it at the mirror. "But we promised ourselves we would try to find and watch over their little boy, their little Abram!"

He sighed. "It has taken us 50 years to find him, if it's truly him. We must keep our promise to ourselves, if only for the sake of what his mother and father suffered at the hands of the Nazis! I must tell him! His parents are long dead. He never knew them! I am the closest he has to a father.

"John Greenwood must know that he is a Jew!"

CHAPTER SIX:
THE GIRL IN THE
CONFESSIONAL

John sat straight up in bed, barely able to stifle the scream he felt boiling up out of his lungs.

He'd had the nightmare again, the third time since he'd come back from Denver a week ago, and he was utterly exhausted, shaking all over, heart pounding, pillow and T-shirt and boxer shorts he slept in soaked with sweat. Usually he was only troubled by it once or twice a year. It had been this experience that had driven him, as a young man, to seek the sheltering arms of Christ that had been offered him in the dream.

The worst of it was knowing that this wasn't the last time it would happen. He glanced at his bedside clock radio. Correction: the worst was having it wake him up ten minutes before the time his alarm was set for.

Resigned, he rolled over and put his feet on the floor—it was cold—flipped the alarm off, turned on the radio, and plodded to the bathroom, then to the kitchen where he performed a routine with Mr. Coffee that he could have done correctly in his sleep. Caffeine, and the act of sorting out his morning pills, completed his waking-up exercises. Somebody—probably a great sage—had once said that if you're over 50 and you wake up and nothing hurts, it's because you're dead. The same was true if you didn't have any pills to take. His were for blood pressure and to prevent a slight cardiac arhythmia he was prone to. (He reminded himself to make that echocardiogram appointment his doctor had been nagging him about.) Give him another five years and he'd be taking pills for Type II diabetes like his dad.

He heated up a raised doughnut in the microwave to go with his coffee and pills and sat at the kitchen table listening to the radio. They were running one of Limbaugh's two-minute items which he nearly always found intensely irritating— just the right thing to blow away the remnants of nightmare from his mind. Contentedly annoyed, he treated himself to another doughnut and listened to the news.

One item was of particular interest. The initial announcement to the press concerning Chicago's UN Appreciation Week had been made jointly by the offices of the mayor and Bishop Camelle. The Japanese ambassador was mentioned and, to his surprise, so was John, however briefly, as one of the principal organizers.

Well what do you know, he thought. A feather in his cap already.

A shower and a shave later, and he was prepared to face the day.

"Bless me, Father, for I have sinned. It's been about six months since my last confession."

The voice was female, young, perhaps in her mid-20s, and from the midwest. From what little she'd said so far, she was well-spoken, intelligent, and very troubled. As gently as he could, John encouraged her to go on with her confession.

"I'm a computer programmer, Father. I work here in Chicago for a licensing bureau of the State of Illinois. Father, for the past two years, I've been deliberately sabotaging the records of the agency I work for, removing maybe a couple thousand gun owners from the registration lists."

John blinked. It wasn't often that something told him in this little booth could shock him. "Gun owners? But my child, we need to know who these people are! Why in heaven's name would you do something like that?"

She sighed deeply, almost wearily, and as if wondering now whether she'd done the right thing coming here after all. "Because I believe that obedience to the Bill of Rights—the highest law of the land, Father—is more important than obedience to any lesser laws that contradict it."

"I see, so you're committing an act of civil disobedience, then." He could handle this. He'd committed plenty of civil disobedience himself in the old days. He liked to think it had helped to end a war. But this was different: guns were the *implements* of war.

"No, Father," she replied. "I don't care if anybody ever knows what I've done, I'm not part of a movement or anything. The Second Amendment says 'the right of the people to keep and bear arms shall not be infringed". I looked up 'infringed'. It means messed with, even a little, especially a little bit at a time. Father, there are over 20,000 laws in this country that do exactly that!"

Half a hundred counter-arguments came to mind at once, but the confessional was no place for a political debate. Instead, he simply asked, "Isn't that for wiser heads to decide? The courts, maybe?"

Suddenly, despite his convictions regarding guns and other tools of violence, John felt terribly like a hypocrite. Whatever the content of this young woman's beliefs (he had no doubt he'd find it morally repulsive; she was probably a Randist or something like that), she obviously felt what she felt passionately. He remembered all too well the same passion he'd felt over Lyndon Johnson's war—and the patronizing nonsense that had been finger-shaken at him when he was her age, about his opposition to it.

He should never have called her "my child". He'd felt like an old man when he got up this morning. Now he *knew* he was an old man and that he'd come shamefully around a full 180 degrees.

"It should be, Father, but they've failed."

It took John a moment to recall that they'd been talking about the courts. It was difficult to dispute with her—if he'd been inclined to do so— about the nation's courts. Although he himself was more concerned about a different range of issues, more and more the courts seemed to be the worst sinkholes in a system already festering with depravity. Sometimes he even found himself thinking that the phrase "hanging judge" had been taken entirely the wrong way.

She was going on. "They always rule against the individual these days. They don't care about the law. Besides, these records will be used sooner or later to confiscate people's guns, they way they were in New York a few years ago or in England and Australia just recently. The politicians promised it would never happen, but then it did. I'm making sure they keep their word here."

"But people don't need guns," he said, breaking his resolve not to debate with her, "they only make things worse. Maybe they did 200 years ago, with the British and wild animals and Native Americans and all, but we have police, the telephone—"

"Nine-one-one's a fraud, Father. 'Dial it and die.' It takes the cops 10 times as long to get there as is does for somebody to rape and kill you. Even if it didn't, the courts have decreed that there isn't any legal right to police protection, anyway. If you listen to them, if you're attacked, you have a legal obligation to die—just be nice and quiet about it, so you won't disturb anybody. And that's what people do, Father, they die, because the mayor, the city and county government, the governor, the legislature all think it's just fine if *they* decide to violate the highest law of the land—but we have to mindlessly obey any piece of illegal trash they pass or else."

"So what happens," he asked, shocked at the pragmatic turn his mind had suddenly taken. It was like the old days when he'd plotted with friends to break into the Selective Service offices and destroy the files (not all that different an act from the one she'd committed) or find some vandalism they could inflict on the ROTC program. "What happens when someone is caught with a firearm, tells the cops it's registered, but the message comes back that it isn't? Who have you helped then?"

"Oh, I thought of that!" She stirred on the other side of the screen and took a deep breath. Now there was pride and excitement in her voice. In her mind, she wasn't a committing a heinously criminal act, but performing a good deed of the same kind he and his friends had been convinced they were performing. And if it broke a law, well, there were higher laws to be acknowledged, weren't there?

But ... *guns*?

Unaware of the moral and emotional turmoil she was causing on the other side of the booth, she continued. "I fixed it so the system can be accessed only one way. I encrypted each registration so it can only be decrypted if you know who you're looking up. To read a person's record, you need his name and social security number. These produce a key that, unknown to you, unlocks the person's record. But there's no way, short of a supercomputer running constantly for thousands of years, to decrypt all the millions of gun owner records. You can still get stats from the data—you can find out how many registered gun owners live in Gifford, Illinois—but you can't find out who they are because that information is encrypted. Remember I said I'm a computer programmer? Well, Father, I'm a *good* programmer."

"Tell me," he asked, trying with all his might to remain calm. "If you're certain that you're in the right, why have you come to me?"

"Because I'm worried about my honor, Father. See, I'm breaking my word to my employers, bags of human waste in $500 suits that they may—oh, I'm sorry, Father! I just mean that they don't care who dies, and I know they're going to eventually break their word to the people of Illinois. It's hard to sort out which is the greater moral imperative here—and what's the lesser of two evils."

John sat back in thought. His initial impulse had been to tell her to turn herself over to the authorities immediately. What she'd done, what she'd been doing for two years, was utterly reprehensible. But he also knew that when he began using words like "utterly" and "reprehensible", he was being a stuffed shirt instead of a good priest. What's more, this was the first time in a long while he'd heard a young person use the word "honor" that way.

But it wasn't the first such instance of sabotage he'd heard in this confessional.

The last one had been an IRS employee.

They seemed to be growing more frequent all the time.

Rather perfunctorily, he set her a mild penance and told her to go and sin no more. If a priest had told him that 30 years ago, back in 1968, would it have deterred him for an instant from some act of civil disobedience aimed at ending an evil war?

Inwardly, he chuckled. He disagreed with his young parishioner, but her convictions were no less strongly held than his had been—or still were, for that matter.

Something to think about as he got ready for the daily Mass.

Or possibly avoid thinking about altogether.

"But I must see him now!"

"But you don't have an appointment!"

I refuse to leave until I talk to him!"

John's concentration broke. He looked up from the paperwork that was the first chore associated with UN Appreciation Day in March—the bishop's aide had dropped off about ten pounds of it, along with a note from Camelle himself that could be read as encouraging or threatening with equal ease and accuracy. Daily confessions, two masses, and lunch were over with. The voices had come from the outer office—he had his door shut so they'd been a bit muffled—but he thought he recognized the one that wasn't Eleanor's.

He'd already been interrupted enough this afternoon. Sheila Hensley—make that Sheila Gibbs—had finally caught him on the phone, and he'd enjoyed the conversation far more than he wanted to admit to himself. She'd always had a regrettably sexy voice. No sooner had he hung up then Kitch had called to make an appointment for lunch later in the week. Growling a little to himself, he got up from his desk, strode to the door, swung it wide, and started to demand, "All right, what's going—"

To his astonishment, his sometime secretary/
receptionist was on her feet, glaring upward over
her desk at a familiar figure who seemed to be
glaring right back down at her. As he'd suspected,
it was the old Jewish gentleman from the cab last
week, Albert ... Albert ...

"Mr. Mendelsohn," John said, grateful he'd
recalled the name but otherwise at a loss for better
words. "Albert. Is there something I can do for
you?"

Albert swung toward him. "No, not at all. But
there's something I can do for you."

John nodded, gave Eleanor a brief, mollifying
look, then asked, "May I take your coat? And would
you like something—coffee or tea?"

Albert set something on Eleanor's desk, a cardboard folder, began to remove his hat, scarf, and
coat, and replied, "Yes, thank you, tea would be
nice." He took his garments to the wall rack, returned, and resumed possession of the folder.

John had put a teabag in a cup. He hated foam
and cardboard substitutes and insisted on a small
supply of plain institutional white cups of opaque
white glass. He poured water from the coffee maker
into the cup and watched it take color.

"Sugar? Milk?" The old man shook his head.
John prepared a cup of coffee for himself and carried both into his office. He let Albert past, shut the
door behind him, nodded toward one of the guest
chairs, and sat down behind his desk. His chair,
upholstered in overstuffed red leather, felt less
comfortable to him than it usually did.

He took a sip of the hot, chocolately liquid. "Nice to see you again." In truth, he didn't feel that way at all—penance later, he decided. What he was feeling instead was an odd, detached sensation of dread which he was doing his level best to conceal. Sweat had started dribbling down the back of his neck, reminding him of his recurring nightmare. "You know, I'm not accustomed to seeing people without an appointment."

It wasn't completely true: more penance.

Albert shook his head. "It doesn't matter, John." He sat stiffly on the yellow fabric chair, teacup in one hand, cardboard folder in the other. "This appointment was made for you over 50 years ago. I promise what I have to tell you will dramatically change your life."

John raised his eyebrows. He wondered if it had even occurred to the old man that he didn't particularly *want* his life changed dramatically.

Setting his teacup on the edge of John's desk, Albert opened the folder on his lap. The papers inside were yellowed with age and his hand trembled as he touched them. The first thing he removed, he explained to John, was a birth certificate, printed in old-fashioned German script, noting what he said was John's unique birthmark.

And stating that John's true name was Abram Herschel Rosen, son of David and Etta Rosen.

CHAPTER SEVEN: DAVID AND ETTA

John stared at the document Albert had handed him.

Almost as an afterthought, he reached into his inside jacket pocket and extracted his reading glasses—small, round, with steel-colored rims, 1.75 diopter, straight from a rack at the nearest Walgreen's—slipped them out of their plastic case, and put them on.

It wouldn't have made much difference if he hadn't. He couldn't make head or tail of what appeared to be the ostentatious printing usually reserved for wedding invitations. To one side he saw a printed box into which a tiny baby footprint had been set; at the bottom, a heavy wax seal with an embedded ribbon. There were signatures in a cursive that was even more illegible than the printing—two little dots over half the vowels ... what were they called, *umlauts*?—and a handwritten comment and rough drawing he assumed concerned the birthmark.

Suddenly, he realized that this whole thing was about that damned birthmark, and nothing else.

He looked down at his left wrist, almost afraid to pull his sleeve back and regard a familier feature of his body that he'd lived with for more than 50 years. Albert, in the meantime, was preparing his next exhibit. He stood before the desk, carefully arranging the stiff pieces of cardboard on the blotter right side up from John's point of view.

"Here are some photographs you'll wish to see, of my sister Etta and her husband David Rosen." Usually, the old man was careful to speak the language of the country he was in, exactly the way it was spoken in that country. This time, for whatever reason, he employed the European pronunciation, "Dah-VEED" as he shook his head in sorrowful remembrance. "They were so young, so very young ... Nevertheless, I believe the family resemblance is unmistakable."

With a wave of his hand, he invited John's inspection. There were three, a wedding picture, one of the couple on what looked like the doorstep of their house, one of them at what appeared to be a picnic in the country. "Regrettably, we have no photographs of you."

Because these people aren't my parents, you old fool!, John found himself wanting to scream into Albert's face. Peer though he might, he could make out no "family resemblance" in the creased, dog-eared, age-yellowed pictures. They were just funny-looking people in funny-looking clothes, a long time ago in a galaxy far, far away.

They were nothing to him.

They were no one to him.

And he was beginning to resent this strange old man's attempted intrusion into his private life. In fact, he found he was becoming remarkably angry, and—for that reason, if no other—he held his tongue.

He was, after all, a man of peace.

Unaware of the dismay he was causing (or perhaps choosing to ignore it) Albert remained standing in front of John's desk and began to relate the story of how his two year old nephew—John himself, if the old man was to be believed—had been shoved into a printshop doorway in the midst of a massive roundup of Jews in 1940s Frankfurt. For some reason John began to feel nauseated. He glanced at his coffee cup. On the liquid's light brown surface, a delicate swirl of butterfat from the half-and-half suddenly looked unappetizing.

Albert clasped his hands together. "My brother Ruven and I watched from our hiding place as Edward Gruenwald, the local printer, picked you up." Here, he indicated John, who resisted an urge to duck the old man's pointing finger. "You were an absolutely terrified two-year-old, telling the whole world about it at the top of your lungs, so he wisely hurried off."

"The Nazis," John asked in a sarcastic, disbelieving tone, "just let him get away?" He was getting tired of this nonsense. It was beginning to resemble an endless evening spent with a life insurance salesman.

"You don't understand," Albert answered. "Gruenwald was no Jew. He wore no armband. This was no ghetto. He was an Aryan, one of the Master Race, and therefore one of those for whom all of this was presumably being done—being done in the name of. And he was going home with his son like any good German, away from what would later be described officially as a riot."

John felt a brief wave of sympathy wash through him as, for some reason, memories of Chicago in the summer of '68 came to his mind—he'd been there, breathing the tear-gas himself—of the Democratic convention, clashes between war protesters and a police department gone insane, and of the way the media had reported it. But when had the media *ever* told the truth?

"A Jewish riot?"

"We had some warning in advance. Your mother and father were supposed to bring you with them and meet us at a place where we would be hidden for a time before being smuggled out of the country. Only they were too late. From the place in which I hid, I watched David set you in that doorway. Then he and Etta vanished into the crowd."

"But you know the Nazis got them?" Despite himself, John was beginning to get curious.

Albert nodded. "We didn't know Edward and Julia Gruenwald, Ruven and I, except perhaps by their reputation in the neighborhood. We knew they were both Roman Catholics. My brother and I believed them to be decent people, not party members. We had never heard of them turning anybody in to the authorities—and that was something you kept track of in those days. We also knew our little nephew had a better chance of survival with the Gruenwalds than he would with his uncles and the partisans we were determined to join."

Here, the old man paused, as if looking inward, to a stream of his own memories: a mere half dozen years that must have seemed like a lifetime. John was aware that everyone who lived through World War Two had felt that way about it, perhaps as their grandparents had about the first world war and their grandparents about the Civil War. For him, Johnson's war in Vietnam had seemed to go on forever.

"After the war," Albert continued at last, "Ruven and I sought the Gruenwalds out, only to discover that they, along with their little 'son' Johann, everyone said, had left Germany for good. People in the neighborhood (what was left of it) told us they had gone to America."

Here the old man fell silent. He went and sat in the guest chair.

John Greenwood.

Johann Gruenwald.

Abram Rosen.

John looked down again at the big cup sitting on his desk blotter and realized his coffee had grown completely cold. Something deep inside him refused to accept this bizarre story Albert was telling him—although at some level, honesty compelled him to acknowlege certain similarities to his dream: the running, the shouting and screaming, and what must have been gunfire from the Nazis.

Could the figure of Jesus actually have been his father, Ed, the humble printer who scooped him up and took him home to a new life? John loved his father very much, but the notion was absurd.

He also realized he was getting a headache— already had a headache—and a bad one. Mumbling some excuse to his guest, he rummaged throught his desk drawers for a bottle of aspirin and, not finding any, was about to summon Eleanor, when another thought struck him: his parents' names were Ed and Julia—and "Greenwood" could very well be an English version of "Gruenwald". He wondered how he could have missed something as obvious as that the first time around.

Albert's voice was laden with concern. "Are you all right, my friend?"

Still preoccupied with his thoughts (and trying to find the the aspirin at the same time), John raised an uncertain hand rather than shake his aching head, but otherwise ignored Albert. That damned birthmark. And what was even more damnable, he thought, his father was the self-made owner of a huge Chicago printing plant— Greenwood Offset & Lithography—with hundreds of employees, an international reputation, and extensive contacts in Germany, if he remembered right.

A typical success story of immigrants to America?

Another horrible thought struck him then: his mother was a retired speech therapist, which might explain why neither she nor his father displayed any kind of accent. An excellent way to get a head start in a new country—or to hide yourself from individuals sure to be searching for a child that wasn't yours.

Why was it that the portraits of Dorothy Day and Thomas Merton, from which he usually drew inspiration, were now mute and lifeless? For that matter, so were the autographed pictures of Rocket Richard and Patrick Roy. The Berrigans probably would have sneered at him. At that precise moment, the headache clamped itself around his head like Caesar's laurel wreath and ratcheted several notches tighter. He thought he might throw up.

Once again, he felt himself becoming unbearably angry with Albert for this ... this *invasion* of his life. It struck him (and for the briefest moment the thought came as a relief so enormous he could feel it throughout his entire body) that the old guy must be some kind of con-man, setting him up—although for what, he couldn't imagine.

Almost anyone could do the "research", he supposed, learn his parents' names, his father's trade. Old documents could be faked. Even the birthmark wouldn't be difficult: he often practiced at the rink in short-sleeves where anyone could see it. The toughest part would have been arranging for the shared taxi. That overly friendly driver, McCarthy with his gun, was most likely Albert's accomplice.

"Albert—Mr. Mendelsohn—you've made a big mistake," John said at last. The words came slowly and at a tremendous cost. He levered himself awkwardly out of his chair, head throbbing with pain, and stood. "I'm either not the man you're looking for, or the fool you take me to be." He gathered the birth certificate and photographs and thrust them at the old man. "I think it's time you left."

Ignoring the items John tried to hand him,

Albert sat back in his chair—he'd been sitting at its edge—as if struck a physical blow. "Young man, young man, you have no idea! I thought I had found you alive, but you are *dead*! Would you abandon your people?"

Rendered almost speechless—and unable to think clearly—by the bright circle of pain around his head, John had no idea what the old man was insinuating or wanted him to say.

Hands on the chair-arms, elbows pointed outward, he peered at John now, as if examining some kind of an insect under a microscope. "You *have*! In your heart and mind, you have *abandoned* your people!"

In anguish, John cried out, "Don't you understand? I can't help you!" It was with an almost inhuman effort that he prevented what he said from ending in a tormented sob. In his entire life, he'd never before had a headache like this one. He wanted nothing more than to put his head down on the blotter and fall unconscious to escape the pain.

To John's surprise, Albert exploded back at him. "So here you sit, Mister Monsignor John Greenwood, in your backward collar and your self-righteousness, unaware of what you've let them make of you!"

John opened his mouth to speak, but Albert didn't give him time. "How the Nazis used centuries of anti-Semitic Christian dogma to stir up envy and hatred toward Jews—where there was already plenty to begin with! We were supposed to be the 'Christ-killers', after all!"

John blinked. His peripheral vision was almost gone. He was looking at Albert through what seemed to be a long grey-walled tunnel. "What?" He no longer had a clear idea of what the old man was talking about.

Albert was on his feet, shaking a finger in John's face. "What do you mean, 'What?'? This ... this *church* you serve helped persecute Jews! Your people! By professing Christianity, you dishonor the millions who were exterminated by those who used its teachings as an excuse! You stand with your back to your own people, in the same church that turned its back on us in Germany!"

Transfixed with pain, John almost reeled. It took an increasing amount of effort on his part not to vomit on his desk. He wondered if he were having a stroke. At the same time, although surprised by Albert's tirade—and queerly unsettled by being called "young man"—he felt strangely unmoved by it. It was merely an unfortunate consequence, he lectured at himself through pulsing agony, of a bereaved and troubled old man releasing half a century of pent-up anger.

And of a particularly horrible case of mistaken identity.

But Albert was relentless. "John, there must be something innately Jewish in you that I can appeal to! Listen to your heart! Listen to your blood! No matter the disguise, *they* are Jewish, and you must admit it sooner or later. There were Jews like you in Germany who thought they were something else, and they all perished!"

Suddenly, there could be no more waiting, no more resistance. Holding up a palm toward Albert—he dared not try to speak a word—he got around the desk somehow, jerked open his office door, and ran the few steps for the little half bath off the reception area. There, having slammed and locked the door, he was violently sick, and when, after a long time, he was finished, his head hurt even worse than before.

He hadn't managed to turn the light on. Now he rose slowly and shakily to his feet, let the flourescent tube over the mirror blink itself to life—there was now an excruciating pain in his eyes—wiped his face with a wet paper towel, and rinsed his mouth out. He turned on the ventilation fan to do something about the sour smell. Happily, his clothing and shoes appeared to have escaped the ordeal unstained. Opening the door—Eleanor stood, her eyes wide open with astonished concern—he staggered back to his office.

On his desk, the German birth certificate and yellowed photographs remained, along with a crisp, shiny new business card. The card was Albert's, of course, and written diagonally across the printing were the words, "When you are ready, call."

He'd added the telephone number of the Piper Arms Hotel across the street.

The old man was gone.

Vaguely, he heard Eleanor calling 911 before he blacked out.

CHAPTER EIGHT: BLAKE CHAPMAN

He was late.

John hurried through the double glass doors of the Eubank Pavilion Ice Center into the warm lobby of the building he thought of as a second home. Here he coached youth hockey three times a week. Except for some recreational skaters and a gaggle of little figure skating girls, the place was empty. His boys would be suiting up already.

Not wanting to brave the crowded team locker room 10 minutes after he should have been there, he chose a public room for changing shared by casual skaters and those who came to use the swimming pool. It was large, effectively partitioned off by rows of battered steel lockers.

John found one that wasn't too dirty for his belongings, sat on the bench before it, took off his rubbers and Allen Edmonds, found his skates, and began lacing them up, an act he'd performed without thinking for more than 50 years, since his dad had taken him skating, later playing hockey, on lakes and ponds all over northern Illinois. Now the skating was done indoors, and the leather and tool-steel skates he'd taken such good care of had long since been replaced with plastic, fiberglass, and stainless. Still, the motions remained the same, and he went through them automatically and contentedly.

Suddenly, he heard the door swing and a couple of people enter. He couldn't see them for the lockers. "Dad," he heard a younger voice echoing off the room's hard surfaces. "What do you suppose that police officer's problem was? All we wanted was directions. Guess the nicest thing I can say about him was that he was *almost* civil."

The older voice responded, "I saw you pick up on that right away. His problem, son, is that he didn't see us as tax-paying, law-abiding citizens who'd simply lost their way, but as a pair of black adult males—you're big for your age, you know— who made him insecure enough to revert to hostility without any better reason."

Both voices crossed the far end of the room as the newcomers looked for their own clean locker. John felt guilty eavesdropping, but he was also fascinated with the conversation.

"That's why I've always worried about your passing your driver's test and being out on the road by yourself." It was the older voice again. John suddenly recognized the younger one as his new goalie, Blake Chapman, whose parents had scrimped and saved, often working at two jobs apiece, to raise their son in a decent neighborhood and have him educated in a parochial school, even though they were Baptists.

"You know, son, it's one thing when that car you talked me into holding onto for your 17th birthday was just sitting out in the driveway taking up space, but it's another when ... "

The boy protested, "Dad, it's not just 'that car',

it's a 1970 Chevelle Super Sport! It's a classic—just look it up on the web! And you don't need to worry about me pulling any crazy stunts—"

"No," the father replied—he'd be Harvey Chapman, from whom John had bought his shoes. "It's not because I think you'd be pulling crazy stunts in a car—I beg your pardon, a 1970 Chevelle Super Sport—you've always demonstrated both independence and real concern for others. You think things out for yourself and act accordingly."

"That's how you and Mom taught me," Blake responded. John could tell from his voice that he was lacing up his skates.

"So it is. You choose your friends with care and don't expose yourself to strangers in such a way as to be hurt by them. Seems like you've always known what's expected of you, what you can do and not do, and where and when you can do it. You've always understood that you're accountable for your actions. You've always understood that if you do as well in school as you do in the rink, you'll be able to write your own ticket, instead of being stuck like the 'boys in the hood' with a no-collar job. You're a great son and I'm proud of you."

"Thanks, Dad." There was no hint of the usual sullen teenage irony or cynicism in Blake's voice.

"You're welcome, son," Harvey replied. "I just wasn't sure how you'd take it the first time, being pulled over to the side of the road by a police officer who wouldn't see the good things, but just a physically well-developed young black man—who happens to think and act as if he were an

American."

Blake asked, "But why would someone from the government that we've always supported and defended either fear us or want to do us harm? And if that's the case, then why should we continue to support and defend it? Why should we trust our lives and safety to such people?"

"It's an age-old question, son. In every race and nation you'll find good people and bad. You'll find people who are driven by greed and people who live just for the joy of screwing over anyone they think they can without repercussions to themselves. You'll find them in every corporation, every profession, and every walk of life."

"And ... ?"

"And there seems to be a concentration of them in government. They do what they do because their deeds are ignored or approved by the white majority. After all, they're not hurting anyone white, and non-participating whites often benefit from their acts. It starts with the police and runs through every level and department of government. Remember how they caught those Alcohol, Tobacco, and Firearms guys at their anuual 'Good Ol' Boys Roundup'? That was in 1995—for 15 years, they'd been selling 'nigger hunting licenses' and t-shirts using Martin Luther King's face as a target."

"I remember. There was a big fuss, but what they never said on TV was that the guy who secretly videotaped the ATF and got the word out to the media, he was arrested on some trumped-up charge and sent to prison. That's what I heard, anyway."

"Why people like that," replied the father, "gravitate to government and are retained in such large numbers is for someone else with more credentials behind his name than me to explain."

The boy spoke. "Somebody at church Sunday told me the ATF and FBI massacred more non-white people than whites at Waco."

"I heard that, too. The situation's so bad that middle class blacks like us avoid dealing with any form of government. It used to be a good way to get a start in life, but minorities come out of the military today worse off than when they went in. Health and housing agencies have the same impact on people in their charge. Prisons are no more than incubation chambers that confine petty criminals just long enough to turn them into hardened career criminals."

"All the while they're claiming to help us," said the boy. John heard his locker open and close.

"I'll tell you what their 'help' is worth, son: you know that government form your Uncle Jake had to sign over in Gary to get that revolver he bought, Form 4473?"

"The yellow thing they gave him at the store?" By now the boy would be suited up as a goalie and only barely recognizable.

"Right. Well did you notice how it wanted him to state what color he was? What *race* he was?"

"Isn't that supposed to be illegal, Dad?"

"Sure it is, son. But what does a little thing like that matter when the ATF can massacre a whole bunch of people any time they want and get clean away with it? What's one more broken law to them?"

"But what are the civil rights groups doing about it?"

"Nothing—kissing up to da massah. Son, they've all been bought with government bribes like Aid to Dependent Children and Affirmative Action. Tell you something else: every gun law in this country was meant to keep some minority disarmed and helpless. The Sullivan Act, after WWI, was to keep guns out of the hands of the Irish in New York. The 1934 National Firearms Act was to disarm Italians. The laws against semiautos passed a while ago in California were aimed at Vietnamese and Hispanics. And the Brady Bill passed when Congress noticed how many women were buying guns and it scared them."

"And us?"

"The 1968 Gun Control Act was passed at the very moment folks like us decided we were mad as hell and not gonna take it anymore. That great 'liberal' Senator Thomas Dodd went to the Library of Congress and had them translate *Nazi* gun laws for him to use as a model. That's why when I decided we needed something to defend the house, I bought my P-38 from a private party and didn't bother to ask anybody's permission. Nobody has any right to tell me no. In fact the 14th Amendment was passed to *prevent* state and local governments from denying us the right to own and carry weapons."

"Gee, Dad, I didn't know that."

"Listen and watch closely, son. We're useful right now, when most of us vote Democrat in big, reliable blocks. But that's changing, and when the man has used us as much as he can—as much as we'll let him—you can bet he'll create a situation and turn on us, put us 'back on the plantation', one way or another. What is it Ken Hamblin says, 'Every liberal oughta own his own Negro'?"

John sighed inwardly. This was just like that computer programmer he'd heard in confession, but this time he wasn't obligated not to turn the boy's father in for having an illegal gun. Bishop Camelle, his ostensible mentor, would have done it in a Chicago second—60 times faster than a New York minute—and insisted on throwing the switch on the Cook County jail's infamous electric chair.

John had attended a seminar once, some social worker from the Florida state education system, who'd argued that families with guns are dysfunctional by definition and require identification and intervention. Trouble was that Blake and his dad didn't sound dysfunctional. They sounded exactly like he and his father 40-odd years ago, talking "manfully" on "manful" matters.

He pulled a pair of spring-loaded plastic guards from his bag and slipped them over his blades. He'd just had them resharpened and didn't want the grit trapped in the indoor-outdoor carpeting of the lobby to dull them. From the bag he also pulled a simple black plastic helmet which he tucked under one arm.

But why did it have to be *guns*?

Weeks had passed since his strange, unpleasant encounter with Albert Mendelsohn. He'd had half a dozen telephone calls from the old man, the most recent all the way from Belgium, and from a man in South Africa who claimed to be Albert's brother, his "Uncle Ruven", as well. But he'd refused to see either of them or even talk with them. Instead, he'd poured himself into his work and tried to forget these meddlesome individuals who were upsetting his well-structured life.

Queerly enough, he hadn't had that recurring nightmare since his argument—if that was what you called it—with Albert. Although he'd had a terrifying moment several times in which he thought that headache might be returning. The emergency room physician had given him two kinds of medicine for it, one was for before the headache (which could be anticipated quite unmistakably hours ahead of time), the other for when it had already commenced. Neither medicine worked very well. He'd found that the headache could be put off with antihistamines, and a parishoner of his, who happened to be a certified acupuncturist, had urged him to drop by.

Instead, quite by accident, he'd discovered that hyperventilating—breathing deeply and repeatedly until his ears and the tips of his nose felt warm and fuzzy—worked better than anything. After 10 or 15 such breaths, he'd hear noises at the base of his skull, rather like milk being poured over Rice Krispies, and the creeping sensation of an imminent migraine would disappear. Sometimes he had to do it two or three times over a period of several hours, but it worked.

Leaving his jacket on for the time being, he closed the locker, left the locker room, pushed through another set of glass doors and into the rink. He collided with an almost palpable wall of ammonia odor that told him a game had been played here this morning—one of the restaurant leagues that met around four A.M. Within the rink, covering the ice, lay a ground fog six feet deep. A product of Chicago's humidity, to John it lent the ice an almost magical quality.

The rink area was mostly taken up by an enormous sheet of well-groomed ice, presently unoccupied, surrounded by the "boards", a low double wall of thick, colored Lucite panels, topped with plexiglass sheets eight feet tall. There were nets at either end of the ice, stretching from plexiglass to ceiling. Here outside the boards, one could walk around the rink on rubber carpeting. High overhead, metal joists and braces supported a corrugated steel ceiling.

At one end of the enormous room, near where John had come in, a garage door showed where the Zamboni was kept. The vaguely trucklike machine resurfaced the ice at intervals that never seemed frequent enough to suit John's taste. At the other end, a huge clock hung on the wall, near a hockey scoreboard donated by a local auto dealer, which sat at an angle high in a corner where everyone could see it.

On the side of the rink where John had entered

was a row of plain painted lockers. Then, down at the "clock end" of the rink, a row of locker rooms had been provided, from which a great deal of youthful noise seemed to be emanating just now. Above and behind the doors John had just come through, stretching the entire length of the room, were bleachers capable of seating perhaps a thousand people.

He was home. Back at St. Gabriel's, Eleanor and her gang of parish moms had begun this morning, decorating the church and rectory for Christmas. Usually he enjoyed helping, but this year he couldn't seem to get into the spirit. He was grateful to be taken from his headquarters by the necessity and duty to manage hockey practice.

Breathing deeply to enjoy the cool air of the rink despite its athletic odor, John plodded down to the locker rooms. He pushed his helmet onto his head, got it arranged properly about his ears, reached to his chest for a chrome-plated whistle, and blew on it hard, three times. The noise penetrated the racket the boys were making and echoed off the cinderblock walls and steel ceiling of the rink.

As he drew even with the locker rooms, he saw that his boys were in their jerseys and protective armor already. Quite a group, he thought. They certainly looked more "like America" than a cabinet any President had ever cobbled together. Maybe a third had that unique "map of Ireland" on their faces, a look that characterized Chicago as fully as if they'd been German or Polish. He also had some black kids, a smattering of Hispanics, and Asians in increasing number. One—Valery, the tall one—was Russian, the son of recent immigrants.

Helmets lay scattered as if after some battle of ancient classical times. Some of the boys were simply standing around talking the sort of talk enjoyed by 15-year-olds: tall tales, "gross-outs", amiable insults, dirty jokes he pretended not to hear. Others were batting a tennis ball across the floor with their sticks in the endless and pretty much automatic quest for perfect control of stick and puck.

The walls in this area of the rink, along with the outsides of the boards around it and practically everything else, were freckled with black marks two inches across and the shape of a new moon, where practice had been carried out—contrary to rules that didn't seem to have much effect—with actual pucks. Others preferred golf balls, although a slap-shot ricocheting off a cinderblock wall at the wrong place or time could mean a concussion or worse.

He whistled again. "Yo, Klingons, gather up the brain-buckets and out onto the ice!"

He opened a gate in the boards and preceeded them. Those who loved the ice as much as he did quickly followed, jostling amidst the laughter of the pure of heart. For 10 minutes, he had them play "kill the goalie", an exercise in which everybody made shots while Blake attempted to fend them off. At first it was by turns. John was about to order the final phase of "kill the goalie", in which everybody fired at once, when he saw the rink administrator coming awkwardly toward him on the ice in street shoes. He skated over to save her the steps (and the ice a dose of grit).

"What is it, Christine?" he asked the woman. She had dark, curly hair, but her usually laughing eyes looked disturbed.

"Monsignor, you have an urgent call in the office—" He was, after all, a priest. It could be a birth, a death, or Eleanor suffering a decorating emergency at the rectory.

"—from your mother." A cold chill shot up his spine. His mother never called him at work. It must have required a lot of help from Eleanor to reach him here at EPIC. Before he was fully aware of it, he was in Christine's office, standing on the linoleum floor in his skates. He'd forgotten to retrieve his guards on the way out.

"Mom?"

"John—no, no, please don't interrupt me, son. I have to get through this somehow ... and then I can ...

"John, your father's dead."

CHAPTER NINE: GARFIELD AND BRONSON

For 40 years Ed and Julia Greenwood had lived in the Chicago suburb of Morton Grove, a clean, pleasant hamlet whose citizens rested at night, secure in the knowledge that handguns of any kind were forbidden in their community. Just now, John was trying to reconcile that with the inescapable fact that his father had been stabbed to death in a violent and bloody mugging.

The funeral for Ed Greenwood had been performed in a modernistic church that was almost a sculpture in itself, although of what, John couldn't have said. Sunlight would have streamed in onto the casket through giant, oddly-shaped stained glass windows, if it hadn't been overcast 24 hours after John had begun—but not quite finished—hockey practice.

Afterward, he asked his mother if the man they'd just buried was his real father.

Julia Greenwood was a broad-shouldered, large-bosomed woman in her mid-70s, her voice a trifle high for her operatic frame. She wore silly jersey old lady dresses and too much rouge. She was a decent person, John knew, a good wife to his father all the time they'd been married and a good mother to him. He wasn't sure how she'd survive the loss of his father, but he was determined now to have the truth, whatever the cost.

They sat now in a corner booth at a Denny's restaurant near the church, having successfully escaped friends, family, and well-wishers. His mother drank orange juice from behind dark glasses covering eyes that were, at the moment, gateways to Hell. John was having coffee and wishing for something stronger. He'd loved his father as much as any boy—as any only child—ever had. He knew he'd think of him, later on this evening, and for the rest of his days, remembering what he'd been like, wishing he were still here to share what they'd always shared. It would get worse until it got better.

But at the moment there was this matter of the truth. Paralyzed with surprise, fear, and unbearable grief, his mother clearly didn't know what to say. Finally, "Yes, dear, it's true, you were adopted. For what it's worth, I know nothing of your real parents. Do we have to discuss this here, John?"

"I learned of it from a man named Mendelsohn, Mother." Looking for a visible reaction, he saw none. The waitress came with a carafe to warm his coffee. He accepted with a nod, waiting until she'd left.

"What I want most to know is why—"

"We were childless," she explained. He'd meant to ask why they'd never told him; she went on with the answer she believed he wanted. It was very like her. "One evening Edward brought you home, so cold, so hungry, trembling with terror ... He said I must ask no questions and that's exactly what I've done, John, for 53 years."

John nodded but said nothing.

"A friend of ours, another printer, forged you a respectable birth certificate. We were able to get you out of the country before things got so bad even we couldn't get out. Your father ... " She paused, then finished in a rush, "Edward's printing knowlege and experience were much sought after. Switzerland, England, Canada—ultimately we came to America."

"Where," John suggested, "thanks to your skills, you and Dad quickly shed your accents and brought me up without one." This time Julia nodded but said nothing.

"Is Greenwood our real name, Mother?"

"Gruenwald. It means the same thing."

"Am I Jewish, Mother?"

Chin quivering with indignation, she cried, "You are a Catholic priest!"

She gave the words an unmistakable German accent.

John returned to the city confused and angry over the senseless death of the man he'd loved all his life. Everyone he knew was kindly and sympathetic. He heard from Sheila Gibbs, of course, and there was none of her usual half-flirting banter, just genuine concern for an old friend in pain. She'd known Ed well. He'd been very fond of her. John sometimes thought his father had regretted, to some degree, that he and Sheila hadn't married and given him grandchildren. Kitch Sinclair had called, too, and they'd talked for a long time—although John didn't mention his encounters with the Mendelsohns.

Bishop Camelle had phoned personally—John could never get accustomed to his peculiar southern accent—sent him a card, and flowers to his mother. Parish women had sent him food by the carload, representing the cuisine, as close as he could estimate, of 17 different countries. The senior lay deacons sent flowers as well, then arrived in force to ask if there were anything they could do to help. There wasn't, but it was what people did for other people, whether it helped or not.

He'd done it a hundred times himself.

Eleanor nearly broke his heart. It hadn't been that long since her own husband had passed away; she appreciated perfectly what he was feeling and struggled valiantly to avoid imposing herself on his grief; he had a need for privacy now which she, alone among his friends, colleagues, and parishioners seemed to understand. At the same time she had a motherly tendency to hover, to which she succumbed from moment to moment, only to correct herself in a flurry of embarrassment and apology.

He'd spent a long time with his mother—his step-mother, if he believed the Mendelsohns. The idea was ludicrous, especially now; he tried as hard as ever to drive it from his consciousness.

He'd spent longer with a police detective named Roger Lindsay. His father had gone back to his office at the printing plant after dinner that night, as he'd done from time to time as long as John could remember. His secretary had found a cassette with dictated correspondence he'd meant to have dealt with the next morning. There were a few e-mails he'd handled himself at his desktop computer. The last of those was date-stamped 11:53 P.M. According to the security log, a night guard had seen him out to his car about 10 minutes later.

Halfway between the plant and his home, something had gone wrong with his blue Ford Taurus. (Although he could have afforded better, he'd been an *X-Files* enthusiast and joked about driving the same car as Special Agents Fox Mulder and Dana Scully; John seldom watched TV and was only vaguely aware—through a process of cultural osmosis, he guessed—of what his dad was talking about.) John's father had contacted the AAA by cell phone, giving them his location and telling them he'd lift the car's hood in the customary signal of distress and wait. They'd told him a tow-truck could be there in 45 minutes.

In fact, it had taken more than 90 minutes for a truck. When it arrived, the driver and his assistant—nobody knowingly went into that part of town alone after dark—failed to find the Taurus. In its place, at the given address, lay the crumpled form of an old man, stabbed apparently with one or more long-shafted, well-sharpened screwdrivers. Death had been far from instantaneous (it seldom is in a stabbing) and the old man had fought back. He'd also been kicked savagely. From the time the last wound had been inflicted, it may have taken

John's father as long as 20 minutes to bleed to death.

Or John's step-father, if the Mendlesohns were to be believed.

Eleanor tapped gently at John's open office door. He looked up, but said nothing. He missed his morning coffee, but hadn't been able to keep anything in his stomach for days. "Father Joseph would like a word, Monsignor, if you don't mind."

John forced himself out of ... whatever it was he was in, and, feigning an energy he didn't feel, said, "Of course, Eleanor, please show Joseph in."

He rose from his chair and walked around the desk. Spagelli nodded thanks to Eleanor and entered the room in a tentative manner. Usually the young man was in and out of the monsignor's office casually, but circumstances were different now. John ushered him to a chair, asking if he'd care for coffee or tea.

"Nothing, Monsignor, please." There was a book in his hand. He tucked it beside him in the chair. He'd been out of the city since before John's father's death. "I came to express my profound condolences. Truly, I can't imagine how you must feel."

John reseated himself, surprised to feel grateful for the young priest's company. "Thanks, Joseph. In an odd way, I can't imagine, either. I suppose I'll really feel it sooner or later, but ... "

Joseph nodded. "I'm like that, never feel what I should until hours or even days after the fact. I suppose it's a blessing, in its way, but I ... really, is there anything I can do for you, Boss? Maybe you should be home, resting, or with your mother."

"My mother's in the hospital," John replied, "under sedation. She collapsed after the funeral. As for me, I've found it feels better to be here in my office, pretending to be working—I only wish I had hockey practice scheduled for today. I never spent much time in my apartment anyway—it's a lot like a motel room."

Joseph laughed. "Vows of poverty and chastity'll do that for you. I repeat my offer, Monsignor. If there's anything at all ... "

After a long moment, John said, "You could give me a cigarette. And by God, I'm going to have an Irish coffee, if I can recall where I hid the bottle. Wouldn't you like to have one, too, Joseph?"

Spagelli's black eyes twinkled. He'd spent three days looking for relatives of his soccer casualties. He'd even lost track of the wounded sister. "That'd be just the thing, Boss."

John got up, went into Eleanor's part of the office, and started one of his double-strength pots of coffee. He'd have to ask Joseph if he wanted chocolate. In his experience it was an excellent complement both to the coffee and the whiskey. Then he returned back to his own office and rummaged in one of his glass-fronted bookcases. There it was, a small, dust-covered bottle of Bushmills, right where it properly belonged, between James Joyce and Robert Anton Wilson.

Watching the younger priest over the rim of his cup, John took a first sip of his coffee and felt it burn its way down. He wasn't much of a drinker (although he was far from a teetotaler) but this was highly called for, and he enjoyed it.

"I'll take that cigarette now, if you don't object, Father Spagelli."

Joseph blinked. "Monsignor, are you sure ... ?"

"I'm twice your age, Joseph—almost, anyway—and I'm as sure as I'll ever be. What are you smoking these days, Marlboros? I used to smoke them when they spelled it right."

He took the cigarette from the younger man who stretched across the desk to light it. John inhaled, coughed once, twice, then felt the nicotine take hold. It was like having his shoulders pushed down, slowly but surely, by giant hands. His head buzzed a little, but he'd smoked for 35 years before he quit, and his body soon recognized (and even welcomed) the old sensations.

"Tell me what else you came to talk about, Joseph."

Father Spagelli started a little. He'd been looking for something to use as an ashtray and had resigned himself to using the cuff of his trousers. But with the telepathy of a fellow addict, John got up and came back with a small, crudely-formed and fired clay bowl shaped and painted like the head of a huge-eyed orange cat.

"One of my Pee-Wees made it for me as a sort of joke," he said. "From the Garfield joke book: why do hockey players wear helmets?"

"Wouldn't know, Boss," Joseph answered. "I'm a soccer man."

"So they won't bump their heads while they're picking up their teeth." They both laughed. "This was meant to keep them in—my teeth, I mean." He flicked ashes into the bowl, then offered it to Joseph.

"Quite a coincidence," Joseph observed.

"Coincidence or synchonicity?" asked John, suddenly wondering what they were talking about. He realized he'd had a little too much to drink and determined to slow down. By now his cup was empty anyway. He took a drag on his cigarette and exhaled the smoke.

Putting his own cigarette in the ashtray, Joseph pulled out the book he'd brought with him. "You asked what it was I wanted to talk about. This is it. Garfield—not the cat this time, but the author, Brian Wynne Garfield. He wrote this book in 1972. It's called *Death Wish*."

The title sounded vaguely familiar to John. He'd been given his first independent parish the same year Richard Nixon was elected. "A movie with ... "

"Charles Bronson," Joseph supplied. "The first of several. Only the first was very good. But this book—it's much better than the movie, Boss, even though Garfield wrote it backwards."

"Backwards?" Joyce and Wilson came to mind again.

"Yeah. He meant it as a diatribe against what they used to call 'vigilantism' back then. What I call plain old self-defense today. But he wrote the other side all too well, the side he opposed. For instance, there's a great passage somewhere in here, about the ethical underpinnings of self-defense. He even derives the principle that nobody has a right to *initiate* force—although they have a right and duty to resist it. The book became the first argument for urban self-suffiency and probably started the whole trend toward civilians carrying concealed weapons."

Was this shock John felt, or merely the alcohol and the nicotine?

"How did it wind up in your hands?"

"One of my young soccer players gave it to me, right after Jorge Valazquez was killed. He bought it at a library sale for 45 cents, so he said. He also said that the hero of the novel—and this is a non-reading kid we're talking about—had the right idea about how to take care of street-crime. Monsignor, I think he may be right."

John's mouth refused to work without great effort. "Joseph Francis Spagelli, what can you possibly be thinking of? You're supposed to be counseling these boys, not the other way around!"

"Except when they're right and I'm wrong." Joseph stubbed his cigarette out. It had been smoldering and left a bad smell in the air. "You know I have doubts about my ability to remain a priest. I can't go on the way I have, handing out the same old tired answers that produce the same old tired results."

"My mother says that if the world were perfect,

it'd be heaven, and I'd be out of a job." John shook his head and sighed. Backwards, hmm? It did sound a little intriguing. But what he said was, "Sometimes the only answers are the old, tired ones."

Joseph ignored him. "My two boys—Julio Apodaca died in the prison ward, did you know that, Monsignor? Seven inches of car radio antenna shoved through his guts. My two boys, your father, all dead from criminal violence—and at the same time violent crime in places like Florida falls 20, 30, 40 percent, depending on who you talk to, because civilians have started carrying guns."

"You've got to be joking," the monsignor almost barked the words. "We'd have heard about something like that!"

The younger man shook his head. "Not from Dan Rather or Peter Jennings or anybody else with a political axe to grind. But scholars like Gary Kleck at the University of Florida, and John Lott and David Mustard, right here at the University of Chicago, have all the facts and figures the networks don't want us to see."

John sat forward. "You know what you're suggesting, Joseph?"

Joseph lit another cigarette, then offered John the pack again. "Monsignor, the kid who gave me that book was Norman Weinstock. He and his dad belong to some Jewish organization for gun ownership—no, not the Jewish Defense League. Although he made me realize that some Jews, at least, also have the right idea. Maybe there should be a

Catholic Defense League, whose motto would be, "Never again—not even the first time!"

The cozy feeling induced by four ounces of heated Irish whiskey evaporated. John was horrified. "Joseph, I urge you not to be carried away by grief and anger! Aren't Christians enjoined to love their enemies and turn the other cheek?"

Joseph nodded. "Yes, Monsignor, but sooner or later we run out of cheeks. I can't—I *won't*—believe in a god who demands that we tie ourselves up and offer ourselves as helpless sacrificial calves to the worst among us, to the ... *goblins* of the streets."

John's head swam. He wanted to shout, "Stop!" at a world that seemed bent on handing him too much to live with all at once. He inhaled deeply and exhaled. "Joseph, I want you to promise me that you'll avoid making any life-altering decisions until a considerable amount of time—and ardent prayer—have passed, and you've regained your perspective."

Spagelli sat quietly for several heartbeats. Then he stubbed his cigarette out and stood up. "Very well, Monsignor, I promise."

After Joseph had departed—perhaps inadvertantly leaving the Garfield novel on his superior's desk—John sat wondering about the life-altering decisions it seemed he was being forced to make whether he was ready or not.

CHAPTER TEN:
THORNTON SINCLAIR

It had to be, John thought, the mother of all hangovers.

And not so much from the many whiskeyed coffees he'd shared with Joseph—although, except for an occasional glass of red wine, especially with spaghetti, or a beer during a hockey game on TV, he probably hadn't had a real drink in five years—as it was the cigarettes. Another victim of the Marlboro Man—the Joe Camel of the cowboys.

He'd barely made it through the early morning Mass—between the pungent smell of smoldering candlewicks and the intimate mechanics of adminstering communion, he'd come perilously close to embarrassing himself in public—and it was all he could do in the confessional to restrain himself from meting out draconian penances, vastly out of proportion to the relatively minor sins that his parishoners had managed to commit.

If somebody like Charles Manson had stopped by to get it all off his chest, John would have been ready for him.

By 11 that morning, when several Coca-Colas from the semi-secret stash in Eleanor's little refrigerator—the very idea of coffee was revolting to him—and doses of Tylenol and aspirin alternating every two hours had combined to make him feel merely miserable beyond words, rather than sick unto death, he realized that somehow he'd come to a monumental decision of sorts.

He only wished Joseph had left him a couple of cigarettes.

"Eleanor," he called out through his open office door. The room still reeked of tobacco smoke and he was sensitive enough that raising his voice—or enduring any noise above a proverbial pin-drop—was physically painful to him (as was any large or sudden movement on his part, especially of the head). "Would you please see if you can get Dr. Thornton Sinclair on the phone?"

"Certainly, Monsignor," came Eleanor's answer, disgustingly bright and cheerful. She was an unmistakable morning person—she was like this even at 7:30 A.M., when she showed up for the day's work singing to herself—he'd just never noticed before how annoying it was. "Is there any message, in case he's in class or out of his office for some other reason?"

"No—but that gives me an idea. Please remind me of the number and I'll call him myself." He looked down at his telephone. The numbered buttons on its face swam and danced before his eyes. His stomach gave a sympathetic lurch. "Better yet, dial it for me and I'll get on once the ringing starts." He was afraid to put his reading glasses on for fear of confirming that the world had been redrawn sometime during the night by Salvador Dali.

No answer. Eleanor's worried face suddenly appeared in the doorway, swimming and dancing before his eyes just like the numbers on the telephone. He wanted to tell her to stop bobbing and weaving, but she'd probably just look at him funny. John correctly anticipated that she'd succumbed to her maternal instincts again. "Are you all right, Monsignor? Isn't there something I could get for you? Maybe you ought to think about lying down for a while."

"Believe me, Eleanor, I've been thinking about very little else since about six o'clock this morning." Surely the woman must know perfectly well what was wrong with him. Couldn't she tell just by looking at him? Father Joseph had called in sick—about 10 minutes before John had intended to, although he'd promised to do the midday Mass—and there could be no mistaking the lingering odors in his office of stale whiskey and cigarette butts. "However all I need right now is for you to get me Dr. Sinclair's number, thank you."

"Eleanor doesn't smoke and never did," he thought, "more's the pity. She might look at mornings a little differently."

Sinclair's phone rang four times, then, after a couple of musical tones, John heard a familar message in an even more familiar voice:

"You're listening to the world's largest and most powerful answering machine. Please leave your message after the tone." Kitch thought it was funny because he used telephone company voicemail—AT&T was his "answering machine".

"This is," John replied, "an official representative of the largest and most powerful Being in the universe. Please get back to me whenever you can,

Kitch. It's pretty important, and we've got to stop *not* meeting like this."

He hung up, having just conceived of yet another wonderful idea. Levering himself painfully to his feet, he made it to the door and looked out at his part-time secretary who blinked back at him. "I don't believe I have any pressing appointments for this afternoon, Eleanor; I think I'm going to take your advice. Please hold all calls except for Dr. Sinclair. I'm going to unplug my phone and lie down on my couch in here."

Eleanor nodded her approval.

He closed the door as gently as he could, made his slow way back to his desk, thumbed the tiny latch on the telephone plug and pulled it out of the instrument. He then removed a strangely-colored bundle from his lower left-hand desk drawer, went to the leather couch, kicked off his shoes and lay down, covering his backside and shoulders with the garish, loosely-knit afghan his mother had made for him a lifetime ago when he first went off to college. He couldn't imagine how a covering so full of gaping holes was supposed to keep a body warm, but for some reason it always helped him get to sleep.

He drifted off thinking about the individual he'd just tried to call. John and Thornton "Kitchen" Sinclair (he pronounced it the Canadian way, with the emphasis on the syllable "Sink", hence his nickname) had been college roomates some 35 years ago, randomly and serendipitously assigned. Over the years that had ensued, they'd enjoyed many seemingly endless all-night arguments over every possible aspect of life and death. Where John was what he remained today, a vaguely religious man with many doubts, Kitch had never had any doubts at all: he was an atheist. To Kitch, as he'd said many times, all faiths were equally absurd.

"One man's religion," Kitch was fond of quoting science fiction author Robert A. Heinlein, "is another man's belly-laugh."

Ironically, Kitch had ended up teaching—the man was a widely published historian and a well-respected Old testament scholar of what he insisted on calling the "Indiana Jones" school—in the same Catholic seminary here in Chicago where John had attended as a student and then as a fledgling priest. John's "momentous decision" had been to share the last several weeks of his life with his old friend and seek his counsel.

Now if only Kitch would be considerate enough to take an hour or two to get back to him ...

"Smoking or non-smoking, Father?" The hostess wore a tailored green silk dress with a Mandarin collar and traditional slit up the leg. The air in the restaurant smelled of Asian five-spice and things being stir-fried in peanut oil. The music issuing from little vents in the ceiling sounded more Japanese than Chinese.

Still a bit hung over, John gulped hard and croaked, "I'm supposed to meet someone here."

It had been, in fact, about 90 minutes later when Kitch had called him back, though it hadn't seemed to John more than 90 seconds since he'd shut his eyes. Eleanor had had to shake his shoulder gently to awaken him. After exchanging greetings and the mutual insults customary to old college roomates, John had told Sinclair he needed a serious talk with his old friend, briefly explained why, and Sinclair had offered to buy him that long and oft-postponed lunch.

The nap must have worked, because John found that, despite a case of mild nausea, he was, indeed, hungry.

The Jade Window was only a few blocks from St. Gabriel's and John had decided to walk, rather than pull his battered old 1984 Subaru station wagon out of the garage. The wind had let up, it was a bit warmer than the last few days, and a benign sun actually shone down on the city of Chicago. What that meant, of course, was streaming gutters and dripping eaves.

Now, he glimpsed a plump, short-fingered hand waving at him from a booth toward the back of the restaurant. It helped that all the walls were covered from the navel level up with mirrors. He pushed ahead until he saw his old friend, took his heavy coat off, threw it in the booth, and sat.

"You look like homemade hell, John. Been hitting that communion wine a little harder than usual?" From anybody else, it would have been the rudest possible of remarks, considering the recent death of John's father. From Kitch it was simply a way of saying, speak your mind, old friend, we're family.

Thornton Sinclair was no more than 5'7" tall, although he probably weighed as much as John did. He was wide and solid, with a fair and freckled complexion and curly red hair, now showing a little gray, in a wide fringe around the top of his bald head. His eyes twinkled as he talked. The man's beard and moustache, which were the same general shape as Father Joseph's (John sometimes wondered if he was the only clean-shaven man left in America—or at least in Illinois) were the same carroty color as his hair.

John thought he looked like the world's largest leprechaun—or a well-dressed hobbit. He wore a tie and tweedy-looking three-piece suit that perfectly complimented his role as an academic. A vaguely Celtic-looking hat with a sort of pom-pom lay on the bench beside him. He'd had that thing, John thought, or something like it, since his college days. Maybe he'd bought a case of them. Every man, he'd often told John, has a cosmic obligation to find *his* hat.

John had never found his.

"Not communion wine, Irish whiskey," he admitted, "and God forgive me, about half a pack of Marlboros. Say, you don't happen to have a cigarette on you, do you?"

Kitch held up an unlit briar pipe and shrugged. "Haven't fired it up in six months, but its an old companion and I find I can't quite give it up just yet. Don't start again, John. You'll only be making an ash of yourself—and lot of government lawyers richer."

He picked up a familiar-looking metal container and poured some its contents into a tiny enameled bowl. "Here—have some of this green tea. Science has recently confirmed what we sinophiles knew all along—that it's good for what ails you. Supposed to prevent prostate cancer. And I took the liberty of ordering you a great big steaming bowl of hot and sour, the Chinese equivalent of chicken soup. Or would that constitute inappropriate humor just now?"

John surprised himself by laughing. He'd roughly outlined recent events on the telephone for Sinclair's benefit. "No, I imagine that Jewish chicken soup is pretty much like a Catholic Saint Christopher's medal—"

"In that it works," Kitch finished for him, "whether you believe in it or not."

Together they drank their green restaurant tea and ate their hot and sour soup when it arrived. It was wonderful stuff, John felt compelled to concede, hot, dark, spicy, earthy, and mysterious somehow. And extremely energizing. He sprinkled crispy noodles in it and ate them with an oddly-shaped Chinese spoon. Kitch had also ordered kung pao beef, Vietnamese lemon grass chicken, lo mein with shrimp, pork, beef, and chicken, and heaps of white steamed rice. He even ate with competently-plied chopsticks.

John stuck with a fork.

The waitress kept coming to replenish their tea. John hadn't thought he could eat so much, but he did, and enjoyed every last bit of it, the little flat red peppers and the lemon grass combining to leave a pleasant burning sensation in his mouth. Toward the end, Kitch ordered a glass of plum wine, unbuttoned the last button of his vest, and sat back.

"Well, you're certainly looking a lot better, John," he observed. "You're sure you won't have a glass of plum wine? If it's too thick or sweet for you, I could always order you some *moo shu* pancakes to pour it over. Think of it as Chinese Mogen David."

"Not very funny, Kitch," John laughed, contradicting himself, and shook his head. "Thank you, no. That way lies madness. I have one or two habits too many as it is—and don't you dare say anything about nuns!"

"Okay, not a word. Although in my madness, there's a method, I betcha." Sinclair misquoted. He breathed in deeply and exhaled, ready to come to the subject at hand. "So what we have here, fundamentally, is a Roman Catholic Monsignor in his late fifties, who's been suddenly informed that he's a Jewish war orphan."

"Middle fifties." John nodded at his old college friend and sighed. "And Holocaust adoptee would be a more descriptive expression, I guess. That's about the size of it—that is, if I elect to believe what Albert Mendelsohn and his brother Ruven tell me."

"Not to mention your own mother, Albert's wife Rachel, and all of her photos and documents." Kitch leaned across the formica table toward him. "Look, John, I don't want to make light of this situation, but you do realize, don't you, that it would make one hell of a Mel Brooks movie?"

John laughed, imagining it for a moment. "Yes, although he'd be better off hiring somebody else to edit it." Then: "But it's not a movie, Kitch, it's my life. And it's not a comedy, it's ... " He let it trail off at that.

Sinclair took a sip of his wine and cocked an eye at him. "It's what, John?"

"I don't have any idea at all of what it is." He spread his hands in a gesture of helplessness. "Not a clue. I guess that's more or less what I want you to help me figure out, Kitch, what it is, what it means, what I should do. The whole situation has been horribly complicated by the death of my father, so I don't know whether I'm coming or going. I confess that I've run completely out of ideas. I *need* direction."

"Now let me get this straight," Sinclair replied. He sat back again, extracted his pipe from his vest pocket, and began absently fondling it between sips of his plum wine. "You want me—a lifelong atheist—to assist you, a Catholic priest, in deciding whether to remain a Catholic or become a Jew?"

"No, no, Kitch. There's a lot more to it than that. I guess I need your help in deciding whether I'm John Greenwood—Johann Gruenwald—or Abram Rosen. It's a matter of identity, and I think the question of religion and culture comes afterward. Am I John, Johann, or Abram?" The final name still felt foreign on his tongue. It was, in fact, completely alien to him. But he'd also begun to feel, given the experiences of the past few days, that there might be a certain inevitablility to the whole thing.

"With all that entails," Sinclair said, rather than asked. He wrapped both hands around his pipe and put his elbows on the table again. The waitress stopped by and replaced their container of hot tea. Kitch said a few words to her and she smiled.

"With all that entails," John repeated, nodding as if somehow giving his oath. He wished Kitch had a cigarette. He looked around for a cigarette machine, then realized he didn't have enough cash in his pockets. Should he order a glass of wine?

Sinclair sat up a little, with his folded hands on the tabletop. "Well in that case, my old friend John—or my new friend Abram, however it turns out—let me give you the same advice I'd give you in *any* case: forget trying to reason your way out of it. In the first place, it isn't a reasonable situation, it's something like what Ayn Rand called a "lifeboat case". In the second, you couldn't handle it, even if it were: you're a liberal, and you don't reason, you *feel*—and then imagine that it's reasoning. Your number one priority is to be true to yourself."

"How very ancient Greek of you." For his part, John sat back now with his hands in his lap, as if awaiting a verdict. "Ayn Rand, eh? I might have known. And just what would that require, in your opinion—as a man of reason?"

"John, don't get testy with me. You have to eliminate this dilemma from your life, in order to get *on* with your life. And I don't think you can separate the matter of identity, of who you really are, from the matter of conviction—*what* you are— quite as easily as you seem to anticipate."

John chuckled. "I was afraid you'd say that."

"I know you were. In this particular instance, they're pretty much the same question. And if I were in your place, I think I'd begin by attempting to learn a little more about Judaism than they probably taught you in your routine seminary courses on history and comparative religion."

"I suppose that makes a certain amount of sense, Kitch," John nodded vigorously, grateful to his friend and relieved to have some sort of direction to follow at last. It was an interesting sensation, momentarily placing one's life in someone else's hands. He only hoped his parishoners felt this way when he counseled them. "Any suggestions where I should start?"

"Yes, as a matter of fact," he pointed his pipestem at John. "I suggest you meet with an old friend of mine, right away: Rabbi Asher Liebowitz." He fumbled around is his vest pockets. "I should have his card here, somewhere."

John feigned surprise. "The famous atheist has an old friend who's a rabbi?"

"Why not? He has an old friend who's a priest. It was Asher who told me about this restaurant. Fortune cookie—or would that be tempting fate?"

CHAPTER ELEVEN:
ASHER LIEBOWITZ

John hesitated at the door, clutching the book he carried to his chest, unconsciously trying to derive some strength or comfort from it. Or perhaps it was intended to defend him like a shield.

It was an odd choice for a Roman Catholic monsignor. One would have been likelier to expect a Bible or a catechism. Instead, it was a dog-eared copy of a textbook, *Religion: an Anthropological View* by Anthony F.C. Wallace, a personal favorite of John's through college days and afterward. He'd carried it with him in his seminary years, to all the places that the Church had seen fit to send him—including a couple where he'd had to store it in a large glass screw-topped jar so that it wouldn't be devoured by termites.

In turn the book—concerning, among other things, the many ways religion (whether one accepted its mystical aspects or not) functioned as the backbone of a society—had carried John through a great many moments of doubt. This certainly qualified as one of them. Taking a deep breath, he placed the borrowed skullcap on his head, pushed the heavy doors aside and stepped through them, into the synagogue.

Earlier ...

The rabbi Asher Liebowitz—somehow, Kitch had managed to intone it as if it were "The Outlaw

Josie Wales"—turned out to be a man remarkably similar to Albert, John thought, despite the fact that the two men didn't resemble one another in the slightest. Where Albert was tall and thin, Liebowitz was broad and heavily muscled.

There were reasons for the resemblance. Both had seen their native country overwhelmed by acts of corrupt politicians that had led to mass insanity. Both had watched neighbors, friends, families harrassed, beaten, rounded up, taken away, and murdered by duly established authorities, lawfully elected by a majority of the citizenry. Both had decided to *avoid* "cooperating" with those duly established authorities, and to fight them with whatever came to hand—knives, guns, Molotov cocktails—until each and every one of those duly established authorities was dead or had meekly surrendered.

In short, both men had killed other men for reasons that they had found ... salutary. That was the word Kitch had chosen, "salutary". John had looked it up, just to make certain, using Eleanor's American Heritage computer dictionary disk: "1. Effecting or designed to effect an improvement; remedial. 2. Favorable to health; wholesome." A common synonym was "salubrious". Both men, then, John thought, had killed other men for reasons they found *salubrious*.

It was this fact that had been uppermost in John's mind when he'd telephoned shortly after returning to St. Gabriel's rectory from the restaurant. Rabbi Asher Liebowitz hadn't been in his office. John had left a message on his voice mail system, asking for an appointment, and mentioning Kitch's—Dr. Thornton Sinclair's—name.

Eleanor had stepped into his office a couple of hours later, as John was deeply involved with paperwork connected with the Church's part in celebrating UN Appreciation Day. Bishop Camelle's office had called to "motivate" him. The stacks of paper, each weighted with a hockey puck—the stack he'd completed and the stack he still had left—had been just about equal in height, about three inches apiece, when Eleanor had interrupted him.

John blinked up at her sleepily. "I'm sorry, what did you say?"

"That there's a Jewish rabbi on the phone who wishes to speak with you, Monsignor. He says he's returning your call."

John wondered briefly what other kinds of rabbis Eleanor thought there were. "That's right, I called while you were at lunch. Please put him through ... Hello? Rabbi Liebowitz, this is Monsignor John Greenwood, here at St. Gabriel's church. My old friend Thornton Sinclair suggested I have a talk with you."

"Old Kitch," came the reply at the other end. "I haven't seen him in far too long. We should have lunch sometime. I'm afraid I'm very busy, just now, Monsignor. We have Chanukah starting Sunday, and the *bar mitzvah* of one of my best and brightest. Can you give me an idea what you wish to speak with me about?"

John opened his mouth. He'd thought about what he'd say at this point, but it was hard to get the words out. "I'm a Roman Catholic priest, Rabbi, here at St. Gabriel Possenti of Isola's Church, as I said. I'm ... well, forgive me if I have some difficulty, but this is all new to me, and I'm sure you'll understrand. I'm 55 years old and I have reason to believe that I may be a Jewish Holocaust orphan."

There was a pause at Liebowitz's end. "Stated forthrightly. Not unprecedented. It would make a great Mel Brooks movie."

John was startled. "That's exactly what Kitch said—except for the 'not unprecedented' part."

"I'm not surprised. Of course you may come see me—better yet, join my family and me at our Shabbos meal this Friday night."

John was amazed. After all, he was a complete stranger to this man. He was not entirely unacquainted with Jewish customs, and their generous hospitality, but intrude on a family at the most spiritually important time of the week ... He said as much to the rabbi.

"Listen, my boy," Liebowitz had insisted. "You're a monsignor, a professional colleague, I think we can assume you won't throw food on the floor or steal the family silver—which is stainless steel anyway. Even if you weren't a priest, my daughters are grown up and have children of their own, so they shouldn't be in danger. You're a friend of Kitch's, and that means there's always room at the Liebowitz table for you. Come half an hour before sunset and be welcomed."

Hardly the words of a killer, John thought as he accepted the invitation, wrote down the address and thanked the rabbi. Still, like Albert, the man had killed for reasons he found salutary. He looked up at the photographs on his walls, wondering what Dorothy Day or Thomas Merton (or for that matter, the Berrigan brothers) would say.

It probably wouldn't be "salubrious".

The table was almost set when John had arrived at the Liebowitz's that Friday evening, and everything made ready in advance. John was aware that in an Orthodox home, no further cooking could be done—it was one of 39 prohibitions concerning the Sabbath—until after sunset Saturday night. He remembered Harrison Ford's—the *outlaw* Harrison Ford's—exasperation with Gene Wilder over not riding a horse on the Sabbath in *The Frisco Kid*, one of his favorite movies.

As the rabbi had requested, John got there (it was only a few neighborhoods away) exactly half an hour before sunset. He'd looked it up in the newspaper.

"Ah, John Greenwood, welcome!" Asher Liebowitz greeted him at the door and shook his hand vigorously. Liebowitz was a short man with a powerful grip that belied his 70-odd years. He looked like the village blacksmith. He and old Albert would hit it off furiously, John thought, I've *got* to introduce them.

"Thank you, Rabbi. I'm flattered by your invitation."

It was an ordinary house (John didn't know what he'd expected) the only sign that it wasn't the home of a member of his own congregation being a *mezuzah* fastened to the doorframe. John knew this small tubular brass object, engraved with a star of David and set diagonally on the doorpost (it looked like a rifle shell, he thought, although he knew they could look like almost anything), held a rendering of Deuteronomy 6:4-9, "Hear O Israel the Lord our G-d the Lord is One," the commandment that this symbols of a Jewish home should be permanently attached to the doorpost.

"Don't be flattered, just come and meet my family, John, or would you prefer Monsignor? My girls are here with their husbands and kids. My own two boys have not yet deserted their poor old father."

"John will do just fine. What do I call you?" John let himself be led through a large living room toward a dining area at the left, two or three steps lower with double glass doors that looked onto a snowy patio. The enormous table was still being prepared. At least a dozen people occupied the room from perhaps age 45 down to age two.

"Call me Asher. That busy lady there—" She looked up from her task at a sideboard as she was mentioned; John guessed that she was at least 20 years younger than his host. "—is my wife, Helen. Kitch Sinclair's friend, John." She nodded, returning to her work.

He indicated another woman, of perhaps 30. "This is my elder daughter, Ruth, she writes children's books, and her husband Daniel, a family practice physician in Skokie. Coming out of the kitchen with that tray of salad vegetables is my younger daughter, Naomi, an editor at *Reader's Digest*, appropriately located on Wacker Drive. Her husband Jacob, over there by the aquarium, is a building contractor. These kids, all seven of them, running around excited about Chanukah starting tomorrow night, you'll have to sort out for yourself.

"And these," Liebowitz indicated with a wave of his hand, "are my sons Meyer and Joseph."

Helen, he thought, looked young to be the grandmother of seven kids. Her hair was up in a sort of middle-aged style, but without a gray strand in it. Her daughter Ruth looked almost exactly like her, but Naomi still had certain teenage sparkle to her, despite the fact that she was married and extremely pregnant—they might be delivering the baby between dinner courses, Asher joked. Both teenage boys were rather like their father, broad and muscular. John caught himself thinking they'd make excellent goalies.

Formal introductions having been made, the rabbi took John down into the kitchen and poured water from a small metal container twice over each of his hands, while reciting a blessing in Hebrew. Thanks to Kitch, John had been prepared for that. He knew enough Jewish history to realize that this washing of hands represented a tradition dating from the destruction of Solomon's Temple in Jerusalem, when the people had been compelled to "take over" from a priestly class that could no longer practice its duties.

Washing one's hands purified and prepared one for further ritual. The table in a family home was held to be an altar of sorts; certain things done at it were substitutes for earlier ritual sacrifices. Nor was he surprised to be given a *yarmulke*, a skullcap representing—not unlike a Catholic woman covering her head in church—respect for God. He put it on, allowed it to be fastened with an ordinary pair of hairpins, and returned to the dining room with the rabbi.

As they all took their places at the table, standing behind their chairs, Helen lit two candles, covered her eyes, and prayed in Hebrew, repeating it in English, "Blessed are You, our Lord, Ruler of the world, the Bringer of Bread from the earth." Everyone sat down, and one of two loaves of braided "challah" bread was passed around. Everyone tore off a small piece, salted it, ate it—John followed their example—and the meal had begun.

"In ancient times," Liebowitz explained to his guest somewhat abruptly, "the priests in the temple offered bread with salt as a part of the daily sacrifice of grain. As a good friend of mine puts it, bread is *the* food that makes a meal. 'You can eat a lot of other foods,' the saying goes, 'but until you eat bread, you haven't eaten an official meal.'"

John nodded. "As I understand it, you haven't made a full sacrifice-substitute."

"The boy's done his homework," Liebowitz declared, to everyone's delight. John had, alternating his research with chapters of *Death Wish*. It was a strange book, especially given its unique literary history, but he found it difficult to put down. Oddly enough, its protagonist (unlike the movie's) was Jewish.

"Before we eat anything, we always say a blessing. There are special blessings for fruit, 'Blessed art Thou, our Lord, Ruler of the world, who brings forth the fruit of trees'. There are also specific blessings for vegetables, for non-bread grain products, even for wine. On the other hand, meat, fish, and dairy products are all covered under a single blessing: 'Blessed art Thou, our Lord, Ruler of the world, by whose word everything was brought forth'."

"I see," John said. "Please go on."

"Traditionally, we begin each meal by eating a piece of bread sprinkled with salt as a direct reminder of the daily grain sacrifice. Before we eat that bread, of course, we say a blessing: 'Blessed are You, our Lord, Ruler of the world, the Bringer of Bread from the earth.' Once we've said the blessing over bread, we don't have to say a blessing over any other food. The Bread Blessing covers all other foods."

He paused to pass a plate. John accepted it and put a small portion of roast chicken on his plate.

"So," Asher continued, "by first washing our hands after the manner of the ancient priests, and saying a specific blessing, and eating bread sprinkled with salt, we've made a simple meal into a sacrifice-substitute. We emphasize that food is a miracle from God by *not talking* from the time we wash our hands to the time we say the blessing and eat the salt-sprinkled bread. The silence gives us an added chance to think about our relationship with God."

At that, the meal commenced in earnest and there was very little silence. Instead, there was laughing, talking, and a great deal of food including a couple of the roast chickens John sampled—and then helped devouir—which were almost indistinguishable from the roast chicken his mother might have served.

Later, Liebowitz led John to his study, where they sat and enjoyed a glass of sweet wine just perfect for a cold snowy Chicago evening. John thought of Kitch's joke about plum wine and Mogen David. A large briar pipe not too different from Sinclair's lay on the rabbi's desk, along with a big glass humidor of tobacco, but the man didn't touch it. It was the ancient prohibition, again, against starting or putting out a fire on the Sabbath.

The next thing John noticed about the rabbi's study was a rifle hanging on the wall over his desk. It was a hateful looking thing, he thought, of battered wood and steel, a military thing, manufactured to do nothing else but end the life of another human being.

He said as much to Liebowitz.

To his astonishment, the rabbi laughed, "You're right! It was certainly never made for target practice or duck hunting. It's a Mauser K98k, a German army carbine of the kind used to herd our people into the boxcars and the camps. But there's a difference, John—"

He stretched over his desk, pulled the weapon off the wall, opened the breech, and handed the rifle to the dumbfounded priest. It was heavy. John had no idea where to safely put his hands. The rabbi pointed to markings on the rear of the barrel. "See, here's the Israeli crest above the chamber. This was made for the Nazis, but rebarreled after the war and sent to Israel. It's cold, hard, solid evidence that they're gone, but I'm here. I've got their gun, and they're dead."

John opened his mouth but discovered he didn't know what to say.

"Tomorrow night," Liebowitz told him, "I'll pass this old veteran around, with its mismatched serial numbers and missing cleaning rod, to my children and grandchildren to help them understand this modern day example of Judaism's triumph over evil. I'll remind them that each pistol, rifle, shotgun, and every round of ammunition that resides in private hands in this country is part of a sacred pledge regarding the fundamental right of every individual to determine his own destiny and resist evil and tyranny."

"Your children and grandchildren?" John croaked.

"My friend, Hitler, Stalin, Pol Pot and Idi Amin all made a point of disarming the people they later slaughtered. As the Constitution's Framers intended, this and all other private weapons are a reminder to those who would enslave us, terrorize us, or dream of genocide against us, of the terrible cost that free, good, *armed* men and women would exact for such folly. They represent a silent promise I make every day to the ashes of my people strewn about the soil of Poland, Russia, Hungary, Czechoslovakia, and the rest of eastern Europe. Never again will we be led quietly, like lambs to the slaughter."

John shook his head, quietly repeating the words, "Never again."

Liebowitz grinned. "I guess I've plunged you into it pretty abruptly, haven't I, John?"

Thinking about Dorothy Day and Thomas Merton, John grinned back as gamely as he could, thankful that his years as a priest helped him now to maintain his equilibrium. "Tell you what: help me serve communion next Sunday and we'll call it even."

Liebowitz laughed heartily, sat back, and sipped his wine. "We have our similarities and we have our differences. Unlike you, I'm not a priest, you know, I'm more of a teacher—sometimes a scholar or a judge. We have very little need for priests. The first thing you have to understand, John, is that a Jew talks to God any time he wants. He doesn't have to 'go through channels' as you Christians have for 2000 years."

"Yes, I knew that." His seminary classes hadn't been altogether worthless. "I've always wondered if that isn't the reason Jews were persecuted in the Europe in the Middle Ages. They made the priests appear to be redundant."

"I believe you're right," Liebowitz answered. "Come to think of it, *you're* the channels they go through, aren't you? Christening, confirmation, marriage, last rites, all that (or its equivalent) we do at home if need be. As a result, it isn't organized religion which is at the center of spiritual life for Jews, it is the family."

And yet, John thought, Jews did have their synagogues, some of them as architecturally magnificent as any cathedral. They also had their holidays, and a rich and ancient tradition which vastly predated his own Church. Sunday, for example (which would start at sundown tomorrow, Saturday night—" ... and the evening and the morning were the first day ... ") was the beginning of eight days of Chanukah, the festival of lights. As always he was fascinated to hear a man speak of his own religion. Sometimes, thanks mostly to Anthony F.C. Wallace, he thought of himself as a sort of religious anthropologist.

"Another thing you must know to fully understand us," Liebowitz contined, "is that the Sabbath is more important to us than any of the other holidays. I realize that this must sound to you like I'm saying that any old Sunday is more important than Christmas or Easter. Well, in a way I guess I *am* saying that. Honoring and observing the Sabbath, you see, is a vital part of the Ten Commandments—whereas those other days are not."

"I see."

"Perhaps you may, someday. It was created by

the Almighty to bring *you* closer to Him."

And with that, and another glass of wine, the two men began to talk, late into the night.

They started with *Death Wish*.

CHAPTER TWELVE:
DR. SARAH
THOMPSON

John stepped through the double doors of the synagogue and, like a shy schooboy, took a seat as far toward the back as he could.

Asher had tried to assure him that this was a Reform congregation, more tolerant of variations, and what Orthodox Jews would consider error, than many another such group. For one thing, men and women sat together here, a practice unheard of among the Orthodox, and dressed less formally. Asher—who considered himself "Conservative leaning toward Orthodox" also considered himself "a fox in the henhouse", bringing the word to those, in his opinion, who needed it most.

The room was beautiful, John thought, made of satin-finished wood which lent it warmth and smelled as if it may have been cedar, a material of scriptural significance. Stained glass filled the place with cheerful light, overcoming the dull gray of a Chicago winter day. In the center, a platform held a pulpit at the left side and a broad table to the right. Behind it, on the east wall, a large cabinet with an elaborately-decorated curtain commanded attention. Above that, hanging from chains, a lamp was fashioned in the shape of flame.

John knew from talking with the rabbi the previous evening that the "really devout", mostly older individuals, had shown up early for prayers recited not as a congregation, but privately. Now that there was "minyan"—ten or more adult Jewish males—the formal service was about to begin.

It started with a prayer. *"Sh'ma yisrael"* the cantor intoned, *"Adonai elohainu, Adonai echad."* The words meant, "Hear O Israel, the Lord our God, the Lord is one." Then, "You shall love the Lord your God with all your heart, with all your soul, and with all your might." Other readings came after that, including the *Amidah*, read standing in silent devotion. It was a strange experience for John, not to know what to do during a worship service. He stood up when the congregation stood up, and sat down when it sat down, as if he'd never been to a house of worship before.

Liebowitz had reminded John that tomorrow (which, he reminded himself, started this evening at sunset) Chanukah would begin. He'd have something to say to his congregation, he'd told John, that went far beyond the usual reminder to light menorahs and enjoy holiday foods, or the usual admonition that Chanukah is more than just a Jewish answer to Christmas. The proper citation for Chanukah was, "You delivered the strong into the hands of the weak, the many into the hands of the few, the corrupt into the hands of the upright, the wicked into the hands of the just, and the arrogant into the hands of those who were faithful to Your Torah."

John knew the historical reference, a hard-won

victory of Jewish forces in the liberation of ancient Jerusalem from the Greeks. Even so, it was an uncomfortably warlike reading, he thought. He felt thankful for the kinder, gentler expressions of the New Testament. The regular service concluded, "May we again be privileged to worship You in our restored Temple, in splendor and awe as in ancient days." The prayer startled John and left him thoughtful, given the recent history of the middle east. Here was a real Church Militant, if its ritual writings were to be taken seriously. He caught himself wondering how a liberal could be Jewish— or how Jews could be liberals. To him, they sounded more like medieval Crusaders—or Rush Limbaugh.

What Liebowitz had called "the Torah service" began with prayer, after which the Ark—the curtained cabinet at the front of the room containing the Torah—was opened and the Torah removed. "Arise O Lord, and scatter your enemies and disperse those who hate you from your presence." To John, the prayer sounded positively Islamic. "The Law shall go forth from Zion and the word of the Lord from Jerusalem. Blessed be He who, in His holiness, gave the Torah to his people, Israel."

The huge double scroll, elaborately decorated, and laboriously hand-written on the parchment skins of kosher animals (animals with split hooves that chewed on their cud), slaughtered in a kosher manner, was the focus of the service and the congregation's proudest possession. Each Saturday, it was rolled to a new portion which constituted that particular Sabbath's reading.

At the moment, it was held high and marched about the synagogue so that all could see it and touch it. Some leaned toward it and kissed it, or touched it with their prayer books and then kissed the books. Many touched it with the fringes of their prayer shawls. A boy, by custom only days older than 13, resplendent in a white satin skullcap and prayer shawl, was a part of the procession. Several people reached to pat him on the shoulder or say a word of praise or encouragement. Others greeted the rabbi and spoke a word or two of approval.

At last, the Torah was placed on the podium. The boy stood behind it. He was Joshua Perlman, the *bar mitzvah* Liebowitz had mentioned. The *bar mitzvah* was a person, not an event, John had learned. What he would say here reflected a year of study with the rabbi and the *baal korey*, who usually read the Torah in the synagogue. This celebration would sum up the boy's life so far, and his understanding of it. Officially, he was no longer a child and was about to formally assume responsibility for his own actions.

Nervously clearing his throat (John recalled the Court of Honor where he'd received the rank of Eagle and his God and Country Award), young Joshua began, his voice firming up as he recited a blessing before reading the Torah portion. It was his first act as a Jewish adult. He'd rehearsed it many times to get each word right. The rabbi and the *baal korey* standing either side of him would correct him if he required it. After Joshua had finished, he recited yet another blessing and then, shifting gears a little, began to deliver his *bar mitzvah* speech ...

"For many, many years it's been customary to begin a *bar mitzvah* speech with the words, 'Today I am a man.' And while I suppose that's true in a strictly religious sense, I can't say that I believe it's true in any other sense, particularly in one sense that I'll return to in a few moments.

"What's indisputably true is that tomorrow we begin observance of Chanukah, our Festival of Lights, a holiday which, in the words of writer and internet columnist Dr. Sarah Thompson, 'commemorates specific historical events, two distinct miracles, and has great relevance for people of all—or even no—religious convictions.' Dr. Thompson points out that, unlike most Jewish holidays, Chanukah doesn't commemorate events related in the Torah or the rest of the Bible. The story is told in the apocryphal books *Maccabees I and II*, which are not accepted Jewish scripture, and takes place about 164 B.C.E., shortly after the death of Alexander the Great.

"Until that time, the Greeks had been friendly toward Jews. They even had Jewish scriptures translated into Greek. Ironically, we know the story of Chanukah mostly from the Septuagint, a translation of the Torah to Greek. During this period some Jews adopted Greek culture and language and formed a Hellenist movement within Judaism, although most Jews stayed faithful to their religion and its commandments.

"Alexander's successors were less tolerant. The first oppression was subtle, consisting of ever-increasing pressure for Jews to become 'Hellenized' and adopt Greek ways. The Greeks wanted Judaism to be an intellectual pursuit, not a religion. A Hellenized Jew was installed as high priest; Jews were required to 'register' as citizens. When that failed, a new tyrant, Antiochus, seized the city of Jerusalem. He outlawed the practice of Judaism, making any observance punishable by death. He also instructed that the Temple be converted into a temple to Zeus, and that pigs be sacrificed there to defile the site.

"The Jewish rebellion was started by a rural priest who refused to sacrifice a pig and urged Jews to fight for their beliefs. After his death, his sons, particularly Judah, known as the Maccabee or 'hammer', continued the revolt. Judah was an extraordinary warrior and strategist. He avoided direct engagement with the Greeks, and instead used ambushes and other forms of guerilla warfare. His small band of rebels, fighting with little more than the strength of their convictions, succeeded in driving the Greeks out of Jerusalem.

"This is the first miracle of Chanukah.

"The first priority of the victorious Jews was to rededicate and purify their Temple. A new altar was built, and a new candelabrum, and other necessities. The rededication was to be on the third anniversary of Antiochus's edict outlawing Judaism. Legend says there was only one undefiled cruse of oil, enough to burn for a day. A week was required to prepare new oil. Another miracle occurred: the oil burned eight days, long enough for new oil to be sanctified.

"In commemoration of these events, we celebrate Chanukah for eight days. A special candelabrum or 'menorah' is displayed, and each night candles are lit, one the first night, increasing to eight on the last. Jewish law commands that the menorah be displayed, visible to passersby, to publicize the miracles and to glorify their Maker. Thus Chanukah is known as the Feast of Dedication, or the Feast of Lights.

"Today, the emphasis is on the miracle of the oil, which is probably a myth, and none on the military victory, which really happened. Certainly the rededication of the Temple was important. But had the Maccabees not succeeded in their revolt, Judaism might have been eradicated. Jews have reason to celebrate Chanukah, but why ignore the stunning military victory, without which the rededication could never have occurred?

"It seems to me too many Jews adopt pacifism as religious doctrine although there's no scriptural or Talmudic basis for it. Perhaps this explains why, though we say on such an occasion as this, 'Today I am a man', it's true only in a religious sense, and not in any other I can think of at the moment, particularly the one I said I'd come back to.

"Today, after 22 centuries, for most of the year except Chanukah, we've all but forgotten the Maccabees, who fought back craftily and savagely when ordered to give up their ancient, sacred practices. The same way, after only half a century, we've forgotten the lesson of our parents and grandparents in Europe who watched friends and loved ones murdered because—despite God's injunction to the contrary—they'd let themselves become part of a culture of harmlessness.

"That's the reason I can't say 'today I am a man'; I'm not free to exercise a basic right enjoyed by all Americans from the 1600s until the middle of our sorry century, the unalienable individual, civil, Constitutional, and human right of every man, woman, and responsible child to obtain, own, and carry any weapon, anytime, anyplace, without asking anyone's permission. I will *never* be a man until that right's restored, until I can defend myself, my family, my fellow Jews, and my country.

"Today, if I wished to exercise my right in even the most limited manner—just as ancient Jews had to register as citizens of Antioch, just as my grandfather had to wear an armband with the Star of David—I'd need to wait five years, until the *government* says I'm a man, and even then I'd need a permit, which I submit is an obscenity, to enjoy the freedom our Founding Fathers intended everyone to have forever, the freedom to possess the *physical means* to resist an Antiochus or Hitler.

"No Jew who celebrates the victory over Antiochus or Hitler should advocate gun control—better yet, call it by its right name: victim disarmament. The message of Chanukah is clear. To keep our autonomy and freedom, we must *act*. Surrender isn't an option. Whining won't accomplish anything. Whether or not God intercedes, *we* succeed only through our own effort to fight for what's right. To do this, we must regain free exercise of the God-given right to own and carry weapons. If we let ourselves be disarmed, like the Jews and others who were murdered by the Nazis, Chanukah will become a day of mourning for lost rights, instead of a joyous celebration of their preservation."

Joshua finished, his impassioned speech no better received than it would have been in John's church. John couldn't actually hear muttering, rather the empty space where muttering might have been. Two people—obviously Joshua's father and mother—sat smiling, nodding with approval, as if only they had gotten the message. This was a Reform congregation, he recalled, meaning liberal, religiously and politically; the rabbi had described himself as more conservative. "I'm burrowing from within," he'd admitted the night before, "bringing the message to those who need it most. I always believed I'd be fired if I spoke my mind on matters of self-defense. Well, I've decided that tomorrow might be a good day to retire."

At last, to everybody's relief, ceremony took over again. The Torah was raised as people recited. "This is the Torah which Moses set before the children of Israel. It was given from the mouth of God through the hand of Moses."

Then the rabbi took the podium: "We are all living today in what the Chinese would call 'interesting times'—if their government let them. Lately it's popular in some circles to draw 'ominous parallels' between these times, this culture, and this government, and those of Germany at the start of the Nazi's rise to power.

"Such comparisons may be valid, but our times are more like those of the Jews in 164 BCE. We have a Greek Empire in the form of a US which, with rare exceptions, has been a warm, open land of opportunity and refuge for Jews since its inception. Indeed, Jews like financier Chaim Solomon helped get it started, while others fought to protect it, elbow to elbow with Catholics, Protestants, and non-believers, in an effort spanning what will soon be four centuries. And just as we have our friendly Hellenistic empire, so we have 'Hellenized' Jews who have deserted the faith—or simply let it be watered down to a point of meaninglessness—so they might feel more a part of the larger culture, and not be socially embarrassed by the 'quaint' customs and practices of their parents and grandparents.

"In a broader sense, the 'Hellenists', the Charles Schumers, Barbra Streisands, Frank Lautenbergs, and Steven Spielbergs, would force us all—not Jews alone, but Catholics, Protestants, everybody else—in the most brutal way, to forsake the customs and practices that made Americans as unique a people as the Jews. For it isn't any idealistic Greek pursuit of truth and beauty we're increasingly compelled to bow down and make sacrifices to, but an evil idolatry of the *state* that views the individual—each unique and irreplaceable human soul—as no more than a tool for its use, an interchangeable part, a cog in its machinery, a commodity to be used in the name of the vile beast-god, then cast aside and forgotten.

"Today we have our own Antiochus, whose evil minions confine, torture, machinegun, poison-gas, and incinerate innocent men, women and little children who refuse to comply meekly with his illegal and immoral decrees, whose evil minions shoot the head off of a mother holding her baby, having already shot her young son in the back, whose evil minions are exonerated of any wrongdoing, given medals for their crimes, pay-raises, promotions, and a position above the law.

"Like the American Revolution, Chanukah celebrates a victory of ordinary people over an army that had conquered the world. I can only shake my head and ask, how much have we forgotten of the true meaning of this feast that celebrates the triumph of freedom over slavery, of principle over mere social pragmatism? How much have we forgotten of events only half a century ago, when that mere social pragmatism led our people not only into slavery, but to a horrible death for millions of Jews and others? Just how much have we forgotten?

"Let me put it another way: what if you happened to be a Jewish law enforcement officer who wound up at Waco—with the background of what the Nazis did to your own people? How many of Antiochus's evil minions at Ruby Ridge and Waco do you suppose were Jews?

"Tomorrow begins our Festival of Lights as we struggle to recall what it was really all about.

Earlier this week, there should have been a 'Festival of *Rights*' commemorating what may turn out to be the greatest event in political history. For on December 15, 1791, the first 10 amendments to the Constitution—commonly known as the Bill of Rights—became the highest law of the land.

"Under that highest law of the land, each of us possesses freedoms that may not be taken away: freedom of religion—the very reason Jews can be Jews in America—free speech and assembly; freedom of privacy and property; freedom to be treated in a civilized manner before the law and neither tortured nor threatened into testifying against ourselves; freedom to have a jury of people like us who have the power, not just to judge the facts of the case or whatever the authorities may say about it, but to judge the very law itself. And most of all, freedom to acquire, own, and carry weapons to resist those authorities when they step outside the law themselves. It is that highest law which our latterday Antiochus and his evil minions continue to violate with greater frequency and brutality.

"It is written in the Talmud, Trachtate Brachot, pages 58a and 62b, 'And the Torah says, *Haba lehorgekha, haskem lehorgo*: If someone comes to kill you, arise quickly and kill him.'

"Tomorrow is the start of Chanukah. But earlier this week, we should have had a Bill of Rights Day, one observed more assiduously by Jews than by anybody else, for we have suffered bitterly over the centuries for the lack of such rights.

"Next month, Chicago will hold "UN

Appreciation Week". Be warned that the UN is the ultimate exercise in 'Hellenization'—examine its history and stated goals. They want you and me and our neighbors as helpless as the Nazis wanted Jews to be. They scream for power to control our children, tax, and disarm us. They maneuver to limit our industrial technology, reduce us to a pre-historic standard of living. They demand authority to reach into otherwise sovereign countries and extract and punish those who fail to comply with their edicts.

"The UN is no friend to Jews or Israel. 'Zionism is racism' they say and the naive among us nod dimly and go along. I ask myself what to make of a people who never fail to celebrate Chanukah—for all the wrong reasons. Who celebrate United Nations Day—but not Bill of Rights Day. Again, how many jackbooted thugs at Waco were Jews? How many in our community gave their support to what happened there?

"It's the hallmark of 'interesting times' that we must all choose who and what we are. What will it be for you? A Hellenized Jew, a faithful Maccabee, or, God forbid, a minion of Antiochus? How many Jews were there at Ruby Ridge and Waco? If you refuse to choose for yourself, you'll soon find that the times have chosen *for* you."

The rabbi finished.

There followed a long, long silence.

Then, Torah held aloft once more, a second parade was undertaken about the room, which would return the great scroll to the Ark. John thought this one was considerably less ... for lack of better words, "warm and fuzzy". The congregation's resentment of what the young boy and the rabbi had said seemed to him a living, palpable thing.

"Meshuggahs!" Someone cried out, to the obvious approval of others. "You ought to be ashamed of yourselves with this propaganda!"

Someone else said, "What's wrong with you? Jews don't own guns!"

Now several spoke at once. John heard, " ... just plain crazy!" and " ... bunch of militia nuts!" as well as, " ... patriot bozos!"

More than one of the congregation simply turned their backs on the approaching pair, shunning the speakers and their message and yet, John thought, dishonoring the Torah at the same time.

Bravely, the two walked through a gauntlet of contempt.

CHAPTER THIRTEEN:
NORMAN EPSTEIN

It had been the longest Saturday in John's life—and it wasn't quite two in the afternoon yet.

First that business at the synagogue. Judging from the hostile reaction of most of the congregants toward Rabbi Liebowitz and his young *bar mitzvah* protege, it had been far from typical of a normal Saturday worship service.

Then he'd gone to get a haircut, something he always did whenever he found himself recalling that old rhyme from high school, "When in danger, fear, or doubt, run in circles, scream and shout". (A second couplet, "And if that don't cure your ills, take a lot of sleeping pills," had been discouraged by the nuns, as much for its grammar as its philosophy.) The old-time atmosphere of a men's barbershop never failed to soothe his nerves, slow his thinking, and let him relax.

Now, back home at St. Gabriel's rectory, he was itching, quite literally, to take a shower and get his clothes changed. Although the sun was shining brightly, it was a little too chilly to take a walk. He wasn't hungry, either for lunch here or at some restaurant. He had plenty of paperwork waiting for him on his desk, he was in the middle of the Garfield book—or maybe he should just drive out and visit his mother.

No sooner had he gotten undressed and into

the shower stall, than the telephone rang. Fortunately, he hadn't turned the water on yet (although if he had, he thought, he'd never have heard the pesky thing go off). Padding across the cold floor of the apartment, he picked it up on the fourth ring.

"Hello, Monsignor John Greenwood here." (In the flesh, he thought, and absolutely nothing else—wouldn't whoever was on the other end be surprised.)

"Hello, John. This is Albert—Albert Mendelsohn. I'm calling from New York to tell you I'll be back in Chicago sometime tomorrow. Perhaps we could arrange to see each other under less ... well, call it *strenuous* circumstances. Could I buy you dinner?"

John grimaced. "Splendid idea," he lied, mentally assigning himself an appropriate number of Hail Marys and Our Fathers, "I look forward to seeing you. Only it'll have to be in the evening—I have masses to say and only one assistant." Then he had an inspiration: "And I have someone I want you to meet, but I have to clear it first. Can I leave you a message at the Piper Arms across the street?"

Albert sounded a bit perplexed—which suited something down deep inside John; it was only fair: certainly Albert had provided him with lots of perplexity in their brief acquaintance so far—but accepted the offer. They said their goodbyes, and then John, still naked and acquiring a fine a collection of goosebumps, punched out the number for Kitch Sinclair.

"Kitch! John! How good to see you again! Come in! Come in!

And this must be Albert Mendelsohn!"

In the short entryway, Asher started helping the three of them off with their coats, hats, and scarves, while John, having struggled awkwardly out of his rubbers, now struggled awkwardly with the introductions. "Rabbi Asher Liebowitz, this is ... this is my uncle, Albert. Albert Mendelsohn, this is Rabbi Asher Liebowitz."

John had introduced Albert to Kitch on the ride over. Now Kitch gave John a significant look, presumably at the word "uncle", which John hadn't used before. John returned a shrug as he and Kitch followed the two older men into the comfortable, carpeted living room. Since it wasn't the Sabbath, a fire was roaring in the fireplace. The windows were picturesquely frosted over, and the draperies over the patio door, down the three or four broad steps that led to the dining room, had been drawn against the Lake Michigan cold and dark.

Each of them was shown to a comfortable chair by the rabbi. They were asked if they wanted anything to drink. Everybody seemed to want hot coffee—John wished there were something Irish to put in it, but it was probably just as well there wasn't—and that's what they got. Sugar and cream all around, no chocolate.

"Now," Liebowitz asked no one in particular, "what's the topic of tonight's discussion?"

They all laughed. Albert said, "Apologies must come first, I'm afraid, Rabbi. The last time John and

I met, I said some rather harsh things to him, and I need to apologize for my anti-Christian outburst. There is history, which is debatable and then there are good manners. I would simply ask, John—I'm not making any excuses, here, mind you—that you try to understand my past experiences and the suffering of *our* people. Truthfully, I have always felt that it was the teachings of the Catholic church that made my life particulary difficult. But you are not a part of that."

"That seems reasonable," John replied. "I'd like to think that I understand as much as anybody can who didn't personally go through all that. I'll try to remember in the future."

Liebowitz asked Albert something about his wartime experiences, and both men were surprised to discover that, as partisans, they had both fought the Nazis, perhaps even side by side on one occasion or another, yet somehow never managed to really meet. It was understood, however, that both men had been on intimate terms with evil. For a long while, they shared war stories that John didn't entirely follow, his mind being focused on the turmoil in his own life.

The rabbi was speaking of his own *bar mitzvah*, held in the cellar of a bombed-out building. The only gift he'd received was a rifle—not unlike the one that now hung in his study—and a handful of cartridges, one of which had been saved and made into the *mezuzah* presently on his doorpost. On the same day he'd accepted his duties as a man, he'd killed another man with his "new" rifle, in order to save his own life.

"But we're forgetting why we're here," Asher interrupted himself.

John wanted our ... what exactly is it that you want, John?

The man inhaled deeply and exhaled. "I think I'd like to ask Albert, if he doesn't mind, about my real parents. What they were like. What happened to them. And so on."

Albert nodded. "That I can do—if I could perhaps have some more coffee." He held out his cup and saucer. John thought he had incredibly steady hands for a man of his age.

"A good idea," Asher agreed, adding, "anybody else—Kitch, would you stir the fire? I'm going to smoke my pipe, so feel free to follow suit. And how about some ardent spirits to ward off the chill?"

"I'd be delighted," John said before he could stop himself.

Once everyone was settled again with their drinks—Ascher had his pipe going, adding aromatic smoke to the atmosphere, and Albert had surprised John by offering him a Galois from its blue packet—the old man resumed.

"Well, to begin with, John, your father, David, was a draftsman, 27 years old. He worked for a firm of architects and aspired to become an architect, himself. In his spare time, he liked very much to read, um, *futuristic* writings, the works of Jules Verne, H.G. Wells, Willi Ley, and Hermann Oberth, and Americans like Campbell and Williamson. He was a broad, muscular-looking man—not unlike yourself, although he was at least a head shorter—but he was a quiet, gentle soul whose eyesight was so poor he couldn't see a foot without the thick glasses that he wore.

John inhaled smoke. "And my mother?"

"Etta ... Etta ... " Albert set his own cigarette aside in an ashtray, pulled a handkerchief out of his jacket pocket, and dabbed at his eyes. "Pardon me, gentlemen. I think of my little sister every day, even—or especially—after half a century. But I have not spoken of her this way, oh, for a long time.

"Etta was the athlete of our family, and I believe its brightest light. She was a gymnast at school, and a runner, strong and swift. I think that in a different country, at a different time, she might have ended up in the Olympics. Etta was ... eternally happy, outgoing, generous, kindly, beautiful. She was tall—taller than David—with an extremely good figure (although some may have thought her underweight in Germany in those days), lovely skin, straight white teeth, and eyes like a doe, with long eyelashes. Everybody who knew her loved her."

John nodded. "David—my father—wanted to be an architect. What did my mother want out of life?"

A strained look passed across Albert's face. "In those days, understand, one seldom asked that about a woman. There were certain expectations as to how she would use her life. Certainly she never expected to be brutalized and murdered before she was 25, before she could have a second child. Certainly she never thought to see her husband dragged away from her, all but blind because his glasses had been crushed underfoot to amuse some thuggish peasant in a uniform! Certainly she never wanted to be dragged off herself, to a worse fate than any of us could manage to imagine over the ensuing 50 years! I believe she might have fought them, my sister Etta. I don't know about David, but I believe she must have struggled and fought."

John's forgotten cigarette had nearly burned down to his fingers.

"And in the end?"

"Somehow they both survived to reach Mauthausen. They were young and strong; they'd make good slaves for a few weeks before they were used up and could be disposed of. It's in the record those Nazi animals kept so meticulously; it's in the monument in Israel. At the last, like millions of others, they were "transferred". They climbed from the cattle cars they'd been herded into at bayonet-point and told they would be given showers. But they were given gas, and once they were dead, they were *processed*—harvested of gold fillings and whatever jewelry they'd tried to hide in their bodily orifices, and then thrown into a trench with hundreds or thousands of other defenseless souls to be buried like landfill—or simply burned, like trash, in the ovens."

John took a deep drink of his schnapps-laced coffee, but said nothing. What the hell, he thought, was there to say?

"My sister Etta, the doe-eyed beauty, and her

husband, the gentle draftsman. If only they'd lived in a place like Warsaw, where they could have taken some of the pigs with them."

"The Jewish Alamo," John muttered, mostly to himself."

Asher asked, "What did you say?"

"What? Oh, nothing." He accepted another cigarette from Albert. The fireplace was keeping the air in the room nicely clear. "Somebody once called the Warsaw ghetto, 'the Jewish Alamo'." John shook his head. "I don't remember who."

Kitch laughed. "It was me, John, I called it that. Remember, we were talking about the massacre of the so-called Branch Davidians near Waco, and how it reminded me of what the Swiss in Basel did to the Jews during the Black Plague, or what the Nazis did to the Jews during the war. For that matter, it still does, especially since the victims who survived were tried, acquitted by a jury, and then jailed anyway on trumped-up charges by a corrupt federal judge in a kangaroo court, and none of the government criminal scum who were really responsible have ever been arrested, tried, convicted, and publicly hanged."

"What I fear for," Albert said, "is the future—if something like Waco can happen in what was once the freest country in history, the freest country on earth. With all the media going along, almost no public outcry, and only a phony-baloney congressional whitewash afterward. If they can do it to Seventh Day Adventists, who's to say that we're not next—again? Or some other group of God-fearing people."

But John hardly heard them, for he was preoccupied wondering about what his life might have been like had his mother and father not been murdered by their government, and what his future might be like if he accepted his heritage. What would he lose? What might he gain? He was about to say something about that, when, unexpectedly, the doorbell rang.

Liebowitz looked at his watch. "I wonder who that could be at this hour?" John was surprised to notice that it was already past ten—and that his host had thrust a hand deeply into the pocket of his bulky sweater. He would remember later that both Albert and Kitch had made much the same gesture. Welcome to Dodge City, he thought.

The rabbi's wife, Helen went to the door. There was some talk from the entryway, and then she followed three middle-aged men into the room. She had not taken their coats.

"Ah," Asher said, seeing them, "I might have known." He rose, took his hand out of his pocket, and, for the benefit of his earlier guests, introduced his new ones. "These are three of the five board members from my synagogue, Norman Epstein, Jacob Kravitz, and Irving O'Brian. Gentlemen, please meet my friends Albert Mendelsohn, Dr. Thornton Sinclair, and Monsignor John Greenwood. Would you care to sit down? I'll get some more chairs. Would you care for coffee?"

The man introduced as Norman Epstein seemed to be the leader of the group. There was something about him that reminded John of Bishop Camelle, not so much the way he looked or sounded as the set of his shoulders and the way he carried himself. "Monsignor, eh?" He shook his head. "No, thank you, Rabbi. We won't take much of your time. We came to discuss your sermon yesterday, and the *bar mitzvah* speech you certainly must have had a hand in. The congregation is very upset. You made our worship service sound like an NRA meeting."

Liebowitz shook his big shaggy head and chuckled. "I appreciate your interest, Epstein, but the NRA is a bunch of cocktail weenies. They're the country's oldest and largest gun control organization, an expensive and cruel hoax—but that's another story. And what's done is done. I spoke my mind and, yes, I helped our *bar mitzvah* speak his. That's my job. What do you want me to do about it now?"

"Well, you could—" The words had come from Jacob Kravitz, obviously the oldest of the three board members. Epstein silenced him with a gesture.

"I think a personal apology to the congregation would be in order next Saturday," Epstein said. "And a new *bar mitzvah* speech for young Josh, more in keeping with Jewish tradition and a spirit of peace, love, and understanding that should come during the holidays.

Perhaps a written—"

"Stop right there, Epstein," the rabbi seemed angry now. Whatever else it may be, Chanukah is

not Christmas. It is *not* about peace, love, and understanding. What did we say yesterday? Did any of
it get through? It's about *war*, Epstein, a war for
Jewish survival! I think too much Charlie Brown or
Elvis Costello has rubbed off on you, or you
wouldn't be saying these pathetically mindless silly
things."

"Well, I think—" Kravitz began again, but he
was cut off.

"Jews don't own guns, Rabbi," O'Brian interrupted. "I left Belfast because of guns. There are too
many guns in this country, as well, and too many
shootings. If you only have one tool—say a hammer—pretty soon every problem starts to look like a
nail."

"You sound like all the political hacks in
Chicago, Springfield, and Washington. They're the
ones who have only one tool: to them, everything
looks like it should be *outlawed*! And the Bill of
Rights is at the top of their list!" Liebowitz turned
to his first guests. "You'll have to excuse Irving, he's
from northern Ireland, and under the bloody
British thumb so long that he wouldn't recognize a
free country if it came and told him his fly was
open.

"By the way, O'Brian, what do you have to say
about the brutal British practice of disarming
Jewish settlers in Palestine and then telling Arabs
where to find unarmed Jews to murder?"

O'Brian opened his mouth, but Epstein
retorted, "Bill of Rights, Bill of Schmights! There
are too damned many rights! That's why this

country is such a mess, everybody insisting on their rights. But I didn't come to argue, Rabbi. I—we—want you to know that your whole congregation is very upset with you, and—"

"I see." Asher gave them a lifted eyebrow. Kravitz was trying to back inconspicuously toward the door. "Then how do you explain," Asher asked, "one of our congregation members who called me this morning to say he'll be joining an Orthodox synagogue because, given the choice between your slicked-up version of national socialism—that's the position that there are too many rights, Norman—and Judaism, he'll take the latter."

Epstein shook his head, attempting to look more sorrowful than angry—and failing. "That has to be Arnold Greenberg. I've heard him talking. He's a worse crank than you are, Asher Liebowitz. He listens to G. Gordon Liddy on the radio!"

"Oh, my!" Asher leaned in and looked him in the eye. "So what are you now, Epstein, the Thought Police?"

Epstein folded his arms and looked up at the ceiling. "Maybe some thoughts *need* to be policed!"

"Spoken like a true fascist. Run straight into the arms of the state, and away from the Bill of Rights, the only political tradition worthy of our people. What is this fatal embrace business that always seems to happen between our people and governments that inevitably betray them. Tell me something, Epstein, if the Holocaust was the terrible thing we all agree it was, then why are 'we-feel-your-pain' liberals like you doing everything you can to make it happen again? It doesn't speak particularly well for your ability to learn from experience, does it?"

But Epstein hadn't heard half of what the rabbi had said. "Who are you calling fascist? *You're* the right-wing loonie! Now you're adding insult to injury, defaming fine, upright individuals—good Democrats in the House and Senate and legislature and city council—who are sincerely trying to make the country better and less violent!"

Asher shook his head, a sour look on his face. "*Hitler* was sincere. As for your fine Democrats— and the useless, cowardly Republicans—in the House and Senate and legislature and city council, the way they act, you'd think Zyklon B gas smells like Chanel Number 5! Frankly, I hope to see the day when all of them—these criminals who've destroyed the Bill of Rights—are hunted down like the Nazi swine they are."

"That's all, Liebowitz," Epstein looked to his fellow board members for support. "You're fired."

CHAPTER FOURTEEN: GANDHI

"Why, hello, Monsignor!" Eleanor looked up from her computer. "I certainly didn't expect to see you today. I though you were going out to the suburbs to see your mother."

"That's what I said, yesterday, wasn't it?" He shrugged out of his overcoat and hung it on a hook. He'd forced himself to take a walk after breakfast, and bought a pack of cigarettes—Nat Sherman's in the red box—for the first time in years. Monday had come too soon for him. Like most Chicagoans, he was already sick and tired of winter—his coat seemed to weigh more every day—and it was only halfway over.

"But she wasn't there when I called this morning, and I thought maybe I could do a little catch-up on my endless stream of paperwork." Having disposed of his outdoor clothing, he passed her desk on the way into his office, then stopped. "You look pretty busy, yourself, this morning. Just pretend I'm not here—want some coffee?"

Before he could stop her, she stood up. "Please let me get it, Monsignor. I'm just cleaning a lot of old files off my hard drive. Four gigabytes just doesn't go as far as it used to! By the way, I wanted to thank you for my new Zip drive," she pointed at the blue, cigar-box-sized device atop her computer, beside the monitor. "It's going to make a big difference."

He chuckled. "Eleanor, you just tell me what you want and if I can, I'll get it for you. Me, I wouldn't know a Zip drive from a zip-gun." Now why had he said that? Too much Brian Garfield—or Asher Liebowitz. "And yes, you can make me some coffee if you'd be so kind. Lots of chocolate, please."

Entering the office, he went straight to work and, as he usually did in such circumstances, promptly lost track of the time. All of a sudden, this paperwork for Bishop Camelle seemed to be going very slowly. Vaguely, he theorized that what he needed was a dose of theraputic ice-skating. Why in the name of all that was holy couldn't there be a hockey practice today?

"Monsignor?"

He was also vaguely aware that it wasn't the first time his name had been called in the past two minutes. He looked up, expecting to see Eleanor, and saw Father Joseph Spagelli, instead. The young man had a cup of coffee for himself in one hand, and was extending another cup to John. What made it seem really strange was that Father Joseph was smiling—positively beaming—something he'd never seen the younger priest do before.

"I'm sorry, Joseph, thanks. Won't you sit down? I'll be with you in just a second." Dotting the last I and crossing the last T on this particular document—an application for a permit for a parade in honor of the Japanese Ambassador during United Nations Appreciation Week—he put down his ballpoint pen and looked up. His right index finger was bent, stiff, sore, and funny-colored from bearing down to get through five NCR-paper copies.

He picked up his cup of coffee and sat back in his chair. "Now what can I do you for?" It was a favorite phrase of Kitch's.

Spagelli's grin got even wider behind his piratical beard. Not for the first time, John was struck by how much the fellow looked like the young Al Pacino everyone had seen in *Serpico*. The young priest took a long drink of his coffee, then extracted a pack of Marlboros, a Bic lighter, and something else from his jacket pockets. He offered a cigarette to John who accepted with more gratitude than was probably healthy. He realized that he'd left his own in his overcoat pocket. Spagelli lit both cigarettes before continuing.

"More like something I can do for you, Boss. You see this envelope? It's my official notice of resignation—"

"Joseph!"

Spagelli showed both palms. "Now, hold your horses, Boss. John. It's not as bad as all that. I'm not quitting the priesthood. I'm more committed than ever to my vocation—it's just that now I seem to have received a special calling. A mission, if you would. I'm finally going to be doing the right thing!"

John took a deep drag on his cigarette, closed his eyes for a moment to enjoy it, then exhaled, and looked at Spagelli with suspicion. "And what would that be?"

"I was at a Knights of Columbus dinner Friday

night and somebody overheard me talking about my two boys, Jorge Velazquez and Julio Apodaca, remember them? That somebody turned out to be the guest speaker, a Mr. James Louis, Executive Director of something called the Ralston Foundation. He asked what I would have done, if I could, to prevent those two shootings, so I told him. And—like *that*; I couldn't believe it—he agreed to fund me for a year, and thereafter for five years, if my ideas work out."

"Your ideas?" John felt a something like chill go down his spine. "Does this have something to do with that novel you left here, *Death Wish*?" He told Spagelli how, despite himself, he'd been working his way slowly through it, mostly in the bathroom, and in bed before going to sleep. He'd found it to be oddly entertaining and didn't quite know what to make of it. He was no longer sure with whom he could discuss it safely.

Joseph grinned. "In a way it has to do with *Death Wish*. You've really been reading it? But it has a lot more to do with those social scientists I told you about, Gary Kleck in Florida, and John Lott and David Mustard at the University of Chicago. I guess the simplest way to sum their findings up is with the title of Lott's book, *More Guns, Less Crime*. On that principle—and against all current social and political trends—I'm going to be paid to organize and oversee the teaching of self-defense skills to inner city youth, including the safe and effective use of firearms."

"*What?*" John sat up suddenly, nearly spilling

his coffee and scattering cigarette ashes across his desk.

"Sure." Joseph smiled and spread his arms. "The kids will learn Tae Kwon Do in a *dojang* here in the city, and they'll be bussed out to a shooting range in a suburb where the Second Amendment hasn't been repealed yet, for shooting classes, once a week. Think of it as urban Boy Scouts."

"Frankly, Joseph ... " John got up from his desk, went briefly into the front room, raised his eyebrows as he passed Eleanor, who was staring a little too intently at her screen, retrieved his cigarettes, returned, and sat down again. Briefly, he wondered how the media were going to react to a Catholic priest teaching firearms courses to former gang members. "Frankly I don't see how that's going to help anything. In my experience—"

He was interrupted as the front door opened— the blinds on the door swung and rattled the way he hated—and a familiar figure entered.

"Mother!" John said. He could hardly bring himself to think of her in any other way, and couldn't think of any reason he shouldn't. Getting up again, he went to meet her. "What brings you here? I think this breaks all precedent. I believe this is the first time you've ever been to my office."

"Except for your very first day as a monsignor," she corrected him, a little breathlessly. "Well, I just thought I'd drop by. I have something to give you." Julia shrugged out of her mink coat which she hung on a hook next to John's. Picking up her purse, and a brown paper package she'd left on a chair, she let

John lead her into the office where he introduced her to Joseph Spagelli.

"It's a pleasure to meet you, Father," she told the younger man as she sat down on another of the yellow guest chairs. "I've heard so much about you."

He smiled, showing plenty of big, white teeth and all of his Italian charm. "I suspect you're going to be hearing a lot more, Mrs. Greenwood." He glanced at John. "Either that, or nothing at all." He rose. "Well, I've still got some tidying up to do. Very nice to meet you, Mrs. Greenwood. I'll see you later, Boss."

Julia protested. "Now don't you leave on my account. I won't be here but for a minute, anyway. I've brought something for John from his father. John, is this young man's discretion to be trusted?"

"You mean, am I cool?" Joseph asked with a wicked expression.

"Watson to my Holmes," John told Julia, interested to feel that he actually meant it. "Anything you can tell me, you can tell him." (Except for that incident in high school, he thought, when he and Sheila were caught—)

"Very well, then, your father wanted me to give you this."

She handed him the package which he could now see was something flat and heavy inside a paper grocery bag that had been rolled around it. Within the bag lay a roughly triangular, russet-colored zipper-sided suede pouch with extremely unusual contents. John took them out and laid them one by one on his desk blotter: A big, heavy, semiautomatic pistol, a green canvas snap-fastened pouch stenciled "U.S." with two more loaded magazines, and a white cardboard box of Winchester .45 caliber ammunition.

Every bit of the gun was black, including the plastic grip panels, entirely covered in perfect rows of tiny, sharply-pointed pyramids. It smelled of lubricant. On the flat side of the gun were engraved the words, "Property of US Navy". John looked down at it as if it were a poisonous snake sitting before him on his desk.

"Joseph," he said, almost in a whisper, as if her were afraid to disturb it, "do you know how to find out if this thing is loaded?"

"Sure thing, Boss." Joseph hopped to his feet and picked up the weapon. With what looked like enthusiastic and expert fingers to John, he pushed a small round button on the left side of the pistol, causing another magazine to slip out of the bottom of the grip.

"Loaded, sure enough," he remarked, laying the magazine beside the pouch containing the others. Then he did what seemed to John a remarkable thing. Holding the grip in his left hand, he pulled with his right at one end of the upper part, causing it to slide backward, exposing what John presumed was the barrel at the front. But Joseph peered into the pistol at the top.

"No round in the chamber. We'll just lock the slide back and leave it that way for a while, okay?" Almost regretfully, it seemed to John, the young priest laid the gun down on the blotter and sat down again. "What you've got there, Boss, is a 1911A1 Government Model .45 automatic. Possibly the best self-defense weapon ever invented, although I know some Glock enthusiasts who might give you an argument. This one was apparently made for the Navy. There are also pawn-shop markings, teensy little numbers, scratched into one side of the mainspring housing. That's probably where your dad bought it. It's a good gun."

His hands still locked defensively on the arms of his chair—out of the way, presumably, in case the evil thing on his blotter decided to leap up and bite him—John suppressed a reflexive retort that there was no such thing as a good gun.

Julia said, "Your father told me he wanted it passed by hand directly to you, in part because Illinois and federal laws made it a bad thing to mention in a will." Her expression changed, imploring him to listen. "Understand, John, that your father treasured this as *the* essential token of American liberty. And you're right, Father, he chose it from a shop full of war surplus pistols, I think sometime around 1946 or '47, because its serial number was 4201776: the opening date of the American Revolution, April 20, 1776."

As a lifelong pacifist, John's immediate impulse was to get rid of this ugly black L-shaped slab of steel. But it had belonged to his father, who apparently had made a point of acquiring it soon after coming to this country. Funny the way memory played tricks: he could now remember growing up and often seeing this thing in his father's study, occupying a place of honor in a glass-fronted bookcase beside the old man's desk. Sometimes he'd seen his father slip it into a topcoat pocket when he had to go to the printing plant late at night.

And now he *knew* he couldn't bear to part with it. It would be too much like forgetting everything his father taught him. How he wished, that on that fatal evening, Ed had followed his old habit and—but *wait!* Wouldn't such a wish go against everything he himself had stood for, all of his adult life?

In the end, all he asked his mother was, "Do you know you've probably broken the law by bringing a handgun into Chicago?"

She shrugged. "No 'probably' about it, dear. They never had a right to make such a law. That's what your father said. He showed me that part of the Constitution himself. I don't see how you can interpret it any other way."

Joseph Spagelli laughed out loud—then put his fingers over his lips and sheepishly said, "Excuse me."

"And anyway, I always break that law." Julia reached for her purse. "I have my little Beretta .25 right here. I'd never *think* of coming into the city without it. Would you like to see it, dear?"

Joseph was almost blue, by now, from his suppressed reactions to what Julia was saying. Could a man die from held-back laughter? Suddenly, from the outer room, a voice exclaimed, "I would!"

Eleanor entered, found another yellow chair, and set it next to Julia, who opened her purse, pulled out a tiny pistol, and extracted its magazine exactly the same way Joseph had with Ed's .45. What she did next, however, was different. She pushed a lever on the left side of the weapon and the back of the barrel popped up, exposing the rear end of a chambered cartridge. She removed this, snapped the barrel back into place, and handed the gun to Eleanor.

"That's nice," said Eleanor, examining his mother's gun—*his mother's gun!* "Would you like to see mine?" She'd brought her own purse and was opening it before anyone could say anything. "It's a Smith and Wesson Model 60—they call it 'Chief's Special'—that my oldest son gave me a few years ago. He took me out to a range and taught me to shoot it; now he comes by about once a month to take me to the same place for practice."

"But your son is a Chicago *policemen!*" John objected.

"Why, yes," Eleanor answered, "isn't that sweet?"

Father Joseph sat with his arms folded, smiling approvingly but not saying anything; by now, John knew perfectly well that the young priest must have some kind of weapon—or weapons—as well.

"But how can you do this," John asked, pointing into the other room and beginning to feel surrounded and totally lost in a bizarre, surreal landscape whose inhabitants he'd only imagined he knew. "With those pictures of Mother Theresa and Mahatma Gandhi hanging on the wall out there?"

It was Father Joseph who answered. "Boss,

Ghandhi only practiced pacifism as a political tactic. He once said that the worst tyranny the Brits had ever inflicted on his people was to disarm them."

John snorted, "Next you're going to tell me that Sigmund Freud never said that people who like guns pathologically confuse them with their own genitals."

"No, what he said is that hatred and fear of guns is a symptom of sexual dysfunction. Take a good look the next time you see one of the anti-gunners on TV: is this a person who *ever* had an orgasm?"

"*Joseph!*"

"You asked."

"And Mother Theresa," Eleanor added, "was a tough old bird who was very adept at taking evil and turning it into good. She wasn't above taking contributions from, well, say a drug dealer, if it could feed the people she felt responsible for. I hope the Vatican makes her a saint right away."

Suddenly, John had had more than he could stand. He felt like putting his hands to his ears and shouting, "No more! No more!"

CHAPTER FIFTEEN: SHEILA

Blessed solitude.

Until the phone rang.

That afternoon, not long after his mother and Father Joseph had departed—no doubt to compare notes on the relative effectiveness of their favorite weapons—and Eleanor had gone back to doing housework on her computer, John had received another phone call from his high school girlfriend of 37 years ago, the former Sheila Hensley, now Mrs. Gibbs.

After high school they'd gone their separate ways, he to college and the seminary, she to college and postgraduate work, and later to marriage and a family. Now she wanted them to have dinner together and discuss their lives. It almost sounded to him as if she was one of his parishioners (which she was not) in need of advice. He wasn't certain, these days, how much advice he had in him that was worth anything.

Nevertheless, as much out of curiosity as anything else, he accepted her invitation.

The restaurant was a bit more—he couldn't think of a good word—than he was generally accustomed to, acres of white linen, and candles that set the silverware to sparkling. Had he not been wearing his collar, he would have been offered a necktie by the *maitre d'*. One thing that could be said for a clergyman's clothing; it was good for all settings from a caisson at the bottom of the river, to a restaurant like this, at the top of a downtown Chicago skyscraper.

Sheila was waiting for him—another old-fashioned touch. They wouldn't seat her without an escort. He wondered for a moment how they got away with that in these times of feminism and legislated equality—then remembered what city he was in and just how far passing the right amount of money across the correct palms could go toward alleviating the more onerous provisions of such a law.

She stood as he entered the restaurant, and he was amazed at how little the years had changed her. (He'd seen her in person perhaps once or twice a decade since they'd left high school.) Without question, she'd have been able to wear the same clothes she wore back then. She was a bit taller than average, with long legs, narrow hips, a flat stomach, and a very slender waist. She'd been a cheerleader when he'd first met her. She was rather ampler through the bust than the rest of her figure might have led one to expect. He suspected that was why a 15-year-old John Greenwood had first been attracted to her, teenage boys being the shallow and predictable creatures that they are. He also realized that, if he hadn't been a priest for the last three decades or so, he'd still be shallow and predictable.

Strangely, he didn't feel a bit guilty about the

way his blood sang just now at the sight of her. It was good to know those faculties still worked, even if he had no intention of using them. (For some perverse reason, the fact that rabbis are usually married passed through his mind. He pushed the thought away.) Sheila had been then and remained today a honey blonde with very large dark green eyes. Her uptilted nose made her look a great deal younger than she was, and so did her high cheekbones and pointed little chin. So this, he thought, is what a teenage Irish pixie grows up into.

Before he could defend himself, she threw her arms around him.

"John Greenwood! How long has it been, 10 years?"

People were watching. She sensed his embarrassment and released him. Nevertheless, he realized that he'd enjoyed her embrace, and that *did* worry him a little. "A little less than that, I think, perhaps seven. Something about your younger son graduating from medical school?"

The headwaiter led them to a table by a window where they could look down into the glistening streets below, if they wanted to, or across, at another enormous glass and steel building. He helped her into her seat—she let the fox stole she wore slip down around the back of the chair—and seated himself. He wondered if he should compliment her on her dress and decided against it.

"You're cruel, John," she answered. "I console myself that he now has a lucrative private practice in Denver of all places. Said he had to get out of the midwest, although Denver has always sounded a lot more midwestern to me than western."

He took the wine list from the waiter. "I get to Denver now and again for athletic conventions. I think you're right. The current administration there—the last remaining remnants of Tammany Hall, I'm told—seems positively ashamed that their city isn't located east of the Mississippi. They built the silliest-looking airport in the world and spend a lot of time trying to live down a 'cow-town' reputation the city never really had."

"Yes, that airport always reminds me of the old joke, 'Captured by the Indians, her suffering was intense'. In tents, get it?"

"I got it. Sheila, you haven't changed a bit since we were in ninth grade."

They looked over the menu before ordering wine. John decided on a house specialty, mullet marinated in milk. Sheila chose a *filet mignon*. The wine they ordered was a white zinfandel.

"So what," John asked with some trepidation as he buttered a roll and started on his salad, "has been going on with you since I saw you last?"

She laughed pleasantly. "In the last seven years? Let me think. I became a grandmother, thanks to my one and only daughter. And a grandmother again, thanks to my son the doctor. My oldest son's still playing the field. I had my face lifted—no, no, don't look so shocked, dear John! What else is a girl to do if she cares how she looks in the mirror in the morning? It helps me to feel—and more importantly, to think—young. And oh, yes, last month I divorced my husband. What have you been up to?"

John was a little startled, just as she'd intended. He knew that she'd been married to her husband—Harry—for something like 30 years. He'd attended their wedding as a guest. Harry was a long-time member of the city council, a nationally-known liberal Democrat, and an important mover-and-shaker in general Illinois politics.

Sheila poked at her own salad. "You could say our marriage ended for a number of reasons. Our children have grown up and moved away, and there doesn't seem to be much left to talk about. And I guess Harry got tempted by one too many young campaign volunteers. Or is it interns that are fashionable these days? John, I used to be a good political wife and put up with it—not unlike the wives of rock stars—but it wore pretty thin after 30 years. And I just got tired of the indignity of the whole thing."

John put his fork down and wiped his mouth with a white linen napkin. He'd only met Harry a couple of times. He was heavily involved in this UN Appreciation business. He wondered what kind of man could abandon this fabulous creature before him for any other consideration—then realized that that was exactly what he himself had done, nearly 40 years ago.

"Are you telling me this as a priest, Sheila, or as an old friend? If I were your priest, I'd remind you that marriage is a sacred and unbreakable bond, and that we're not put here on earth for the sake of our dignity, but to do God's work, even—or perhaps especially—when it isn't easy or pleasant."

The waiter brought their food, so they had a moment when they couldn't speak of private things. Then, as she picked up her knife and fork, and he began to explore the mullet, she asked, "And what would you tell me as an old friend?"

He'd been expecting that. This time, when she used the word "friend" there was a lot more to it. Despite himself, his mind went back a lifetime to dances, ballgames, and hot, steamy evenings in the back of a Studebaker sedan. "I'd ask you—God forgive me—why you put up with it for so long."

"Well, oddly enough," she answered, "it was politics. As I said, I tried to be a good political wife, and to keep trying for the sake of the agenda. Politics had brought us together in the first place, during the 'Camelot' era. I was one of those young campaign workers then, and he was full of ideas and ideals. We both thought there was a Utopian future somewhere up ahead, and that we were going to help build it, together. Sounds pretty silly now, several wars, scandals, and assassinations later, doesn't it?"

"We all had ideals back then. I don't think ideals are ever silly. You know, I thought I might be a Cardinal someday." The mullet tasted rather like catfish, he thought, and the dressing was surprisingly like something his mother might have stuffed into a turkey—without the crabmeat, of course.

"You still might make it." She laid a hand over his. "In your game, you're still just a kid. Look at the Pope—look at *all* the Popes." She took her hand away and started to cut another bite of meat. "It was also politics that split us up. After all those years, I came to see plainly something that Harry never could—or maybe never would—see."

"Tell me what that was—I'm feeling rather short of insights myself, just now. That's speaking as an old friend, of course. As a priest I'm just chock full of insights."

She laughed again, and it was a very pleasant thing to hear and see. "Oh, it's simple, really. The last thing Chicago, Illinois, or America need is more socialism. So-called liberal policies—left wing policies—have all but destroyed whole populations, as surely as if the Democratic Party were deliberately committing genocide. If you read Charles Murray, or black observers as diverse as Alan Keyes or Ken Hamblin or Thomas Sowell or Walter Williams, you come to see that it's so-called liberalism that's filled our streets with bastard children, drugs, crime, fear, and hatred."

John sat back, speechless—a condition he was rapidly growing weary of—his delicious and expensive food getting cold as he struggled with his thoughts and feelings. What was happening to everyone around him? Were they just getting old, sliding over to the right as their joints stiffened and their flesh began to sag? Was this a natural, unavoidable course? His mother was in her 70s, he thought, like Albert and Asher, so they had an excuse. Eleanor was in her 60s. Kitch was the same age he was. But what about Joseph?

"But most of all, it was this—" Preoccupied with her own concerns, Sheila had failed to notice his internal struggle, and was going on. She glanced around them—they were sitting in a relatively secluded corner of the restaurant and by now the winter sun had set—and then opened her clutch purse and passed it to him.

The light was just right. Inside Sheila's purse, John glimpsed the blued steel surfaces of a tiny automatic pistol. He just had time to read, "Kahr K9" on the slide before he hastily handed the purse back to her.

Sheila's voice was low and fierce. "They *created* the crime, liberals did, and then they wouldn't let us deal with it. Their collectivized cops-and-robbers approach—to the mess they'd made—failed utterly and they forbade an individualistic one. But the tide is turning now—or should I say the paradigm is shifting—whether they're willing to let it or not. And I don't have to worry about crime, any more."

He swallowed a drink of wine and shook his head. "You sound like you've been reading too much Ayn Rand, Sheila."

"Not at all. A lady named Paxton Quigley and a book called *Armed & Female*—the perfect antidote to Sarah Brady, Diane Feinstein, Diana DeGette, Carolyn Maloney, and all those other dogooder broads who are only in it for the power. In some ways, Quigley had pretty much the same experience in liberal politics—she was a member of HCI—the same slow but undeniable change of attitude that I did.

"And what does this have to do," John asked, taking a sip of wine, "with you and Harry?"

"Harry didn't want me—he didn't want *any* woman—to have the feeling of security this little nine millimeter pistol gives me. He keeps voting for stricter and stricter gun control—'victim disarmament' the pro-gun side has started calling it, and I agree—even though by now he knows perfectly well it does more harm than good. It's almost as if he *wanted* me helpless, *wanted* me mugged, or raped, or killed. John, you have to wonder about the kind of man who wants the women in his life to be helpless."

For a long while, neither of them spoke, and they got a chance to finish what was on their plates. For his own part, John didn't know what to say. He knew there was some truth in what Sheila was telling him, a kind of truth, anyway. He knew that American cities had become dangerous, ugly places, and he regretted that, for he loved living in a big city with all its various attractions—especially nice restaurants like this and plenty of hockey. To him, Chicago was a tough, purposeful, hard-working city, and despite its many flaws—which included a city government as corrupt as anything you'd expect to find in Turkey—he loved it.

They lit cigarettes. John had offered her one of his Nat Shermans, He watched Sheila French-inhaling, a process of taking smoke into the mouth, then inhaling and drawing it from the open lips to the nostrils. At one time in his life John had thought it was very sexy. Come to think of it, he still did.

"You know I've been wondering what to do with my life now," Sheila told him. "I'm not sure what kind of life I want—I was only sure what kind of life I *didn't* want. I've been thinking about moving to Florida."

He failed to stifle a groan. "Where the old people go to become fossilized? You're still too young for that, Sheila."

"No, no, John, it isn't that at all. Florida is where the crime rate dropped because the gun laws were—well, they're calling it 'liberalized', but that's as wrong as it can be—and a person can get a permit to carry a weapon legally. Or I might move to Vermont, where they don't even require a permit, and it's the safest place in America to live. Or maybe even Texas. That doctor who had to watch her parents die in the cafeteria because her gun was in the car, she's in the legislature now, and they're talking about emulating Vermont. Do you think I could grow to like Texas?"

"I suppose you could," he answered, half in horror, half in amusement. He wished the turmoil in his life could be solved with a simple change in geography—and maybe a pair of cowboy boots. He even wondered if she was trying to see whether he might be willing to go with her. He wondered if anybody in Texas played hockey besides the Dallas Stars. Maybe he could look it up somehow on the internet, using Eleanor's computer.

But mainly, as he listened to Sheila, he guiltily visualized the carefully-locked center drawer of his desk, where he'd placed the heavy brown paper package that his mother had brought him.

Willing or not, God's mysterious ways had made him a gun owner. He had to come to terms with that before he could deal with anything else.

SIXTEEN:
JOHN MOSES
BROWNING

"What's that smell?" John asked.

The instant they stepped into the place—a little brass bell hanging on the door announced them—they were immersed in odors he'd never experienced before. He could smell lubricating oil, he thought, and what was probably some kind of cleaning solvent, but that wasn't what he'd asked Kitch about. This was sort of peppery and almost like rubbing alcohol at the same time. John found it bracing, somehow.

The large painted sign outside had said:

BIG ONION SPORTING SUPPLY AND
INDOOR SHOOTING RANGE
"THE MACHINERY OF FREEDOM"

At eight AM on a weekday morning, this place obviously didn't do much business. So far, they were the only shooters here. Past the unattended counter, however, a door was open on a classroom full of women, apparently taking a firearms safety course. The woman closest to John, at the back of the room, looked back at him for a moment. Half her face was covered with dark, blue-black bruises. He thought, in that moment, of the girl in the confessional. Dial 911, she'd said to him, and die.

No citizen of Chicago, Illinois, or the United States has a legal right to police protection.

Kitch chuckled. "I'd say the manager got in some practice before opening up this morning. Mostly what you're smelling is Hercules' Unique, an old, very distinguished smokeless powder highly favored by many handgunners who reload their own cartridges. I promise you *wouldn't* like the smell of old-fashioned blackpowder!"

There were other signs, inside. Behind a glass counter full of pistols and revolvers, the first thing he saw when he entered was:

GOD CREATED MEN—
SAM COLT MADE 'EM EQUAL

It had been written in what might be called old-time western letters six inches high. To his left, above a barred window looking onto the parking lot and his battered Subaru, another sign proclaimed:

BETTER TRIED BY TWELVE
THAN CARRIED BY SIX
25000 GUN LAWS IN AMERICA
NOT *ONE* IS CONSTITUTIONAL

Taped to the underside of the glass countertop was a cartoon clipped from some publication. It was a caricature of a politician—old-fashioned frock coat, narrow string tie—proclaiming to the legislature, **"RAPE IS FUN—WHEN SHE DOESN'T HAVE A GUN!"**

And on a bulletin board covered with newspaper clippings, a header in the same western-styled six inch letters—but on an international safety orange background with lime-green letters that made his eyeballs feel as if they were buzzing—startled John; he recognized the thought as his own:

WHEN HAVE THE MEDIA EVER TOLD THE TRUTH?

Suddenly, the path he'd followed to get to this place and this moment struck John as bizarre, if not downright surreal. What would the bishop make of all this? What was he, a lifelong pacifist, an ardent anti-war activist, and a disciple of the great Dorothy Day doing at a shooting range with his hand wrapped around a .45 caliber semiautomatic pistol?

The most recent step along that bizarre, surreal path had come the previous evening ...

Having ended his dinner with Sheila and bade her good night, he'd come back to the rectory. What a strange meal it had been, steak and pistols, yet he'd enjoyed it, to be truthful, was sorry once it was over with, and was surprised to find that he looked forward to doing it again sometime. Being accustomed since grade school to reading himself to sleep, he'd finished the novel *Death Wish*—what do you know, he thought, a happy ending—before he'd really read enough to go to sleep on, or perhaps he was simply feeling restless with so many cataclysms going on in his personal and professional life.

In any case, he'd gotten up, put on his overcoat (he didn't own a bathrobe) and an old pair of sneakers he used instead of bedroom slippers, went out through his office to the outer room, and sat down at Eleanor's computer. Wiggling the mouse back and forth, he knew would awaken the machine, making the swirling colored patterns on the screen disappear and restoring what she called her "desktop". He also knew enough to move the cursor and double-click on the little symbol on the left that would connect the machine to the internet.

For a moment, he was stumped. It wanted a password. He hadn't even known she *had* a password, like she was a member of a secret club. But he'd seen enough movies to know people usually chose a word that had significance in their lives. It wouldn't be her own name, that wouldn't be like her. It might be the name of her dead husband or one of her children. He tried: fred, no; fredjr (the cop), no; kelli, no; natalie, no; nicole, no; brittainy, no; wendy, no.

Then, inspiration: Eleanor's *grandchildren*. Could he remember? The oldest was Fred Jr.'s little Erin. *Bingo!* The password box vanished and the screen, bit by bit in a way John found very annoying, became the front page (if that was the word) of HastaLaVista, a company dedicated to finding things for people on the "Worldwide Web".

Okay, what was he here for? The Worldwide Web wasn't going to help with his Jewish nature versus Catholic nurture problem. That involved a moral decision he wasn't prepared to make yet. Nor did he want cyberspace to tell him about guns and self-defense—he'd had rather too much information on those topics lately.

Suddenly, John saw that the internet was like a gigantic, living encyclopedia. He could type anything into the search engine's little window, anything at all, and who knew what would turn up, newspaper and magazine articles, scholarly (and perhaps not-so-scholarly) monographs, individual opinions of every imaginable stripe?

Asher had been quite vehement in his denunciations of the United Nations, and that certainly bore on John's own work. Bishop Camelle had practically laid the entire responsibility for UN Appreciation Week in his hands. He realized, as he put "united nations" in the search engine, that he might spend weeks weeding through the resulting 337,335 references. He tried various other key words, "anti-un", "abolish un", and so forth. What he saw surprised him—and seriously shook his belief in the picture of the world he'd carried around in his head for most of his adult life.

In the first place, not all of the web sites he saw that were antagonistic to the UN were run by illiterate rednecks in Idaho or Montana. Many were eastern, urban, and Jewish. Others were put up by doctors, lawyers, academics, even musicians, a populace, bewilderingly diverse—invisible to mainstream media—who saw the UN as a threat to American traditions rooted in the Bill of Rights.

The Japanese, for example—whose ambassador would be a guest in Chicago during UN Appreciation Week—were working through the UN to set the Bill of Rights aside and seize all privately owned guns in America. A month ago—even a week—he might have supported such an effort, himself. But in the light of many atrocities UN military forces had apparently committed in obscure countries in the name of "peacekeeping", it made him feel uneasy. Even more so since, with the cooperation of American TV and newspapers, it appeared to be happening in secret.

Following various "links"—character strings he could click on that took him from one website to another, he found a California doctor who exposed corrupt research in medical journals that declared gun ownership a disease. He found petitions to remove America from the UN—or the UN from America—and a site dedicated to a young military man who had refused to serve the UN, maintaining that his oath was to his own country. There was even an individual freedom movement in England, led by a respected university professor.

And there was radio online! A program called "RealPlayer" let him listen to late-night talk shows (or music, if he preferred), through the computer. What a world he'd missed, never guessing of its existence. But again and again, he came back to those who'd believed the UN was a threat, not just to American sovereignty, but to the very survival of America and its people.

Before he knew it, he noticed that the sun was

rising. He'd spent the whole night as a stranger in a strange land, full of information—and a great deal of disinformation—he'd never had before which put him in a quandry. What should he do about UN Appreciation Week? What should he tell his congregation about it next Sunday?

Christmas Sunday.

"John? Where did you go? There's no wool-gathering in this sport. You lose toes and fingers that way—and the occasional head."

"Sorry, Kitch. What were you saying?"

"I said, think of me as your coach. Don't do anything—anything—until I've told you to, and if you have questions, until I've answered them to your satisfaction, got it?"

"Got it." It had been a long time since he'd been on the student end. It felt strange. He looked at the zipped pouch lying on the bench and wondered if his life was about to change irrevocably.

"Start by making the weapon safe," Kitch said. "Open the pouch—unzip it all the way so it lies flat. We call this a 'pistol rug'. Set the spare magazines and box of ammo aside. Without putting your finger on the trigger, and keeping the muzzle (that's the front end) downrange—thataway, pardner—press this button there, at the lower root of the trigger guard, with your thumb."

John was a large man, with big bony hands and long fingers. His father's pistol felt narrow, somehow, in his hand, and heavy toward the front end. In fact he'd been surprised right from the beginning at how heavy the thing was. He was accustomed, like most people of his times and in his place, to handleable artifacts of this approximate size—telephone handsets came to mind—being light, warm to the touch, and contructed of almond-colored plastic that made it hard to take them seriously. This was cold blue steel and dragged his arm down in a way that told him it was an engine of destruction, as serious as a gravedigger's shovel.

John did as he'd been told—it was difficult not putting his finger on the trigger, it seemed to *want* to be there—and the magazine, long and black, slid from the bottom of the grip. He caught it in his left hand before it could hit the padded top of the bench.

Kitch told him, "Well done. You realize, of course, that the weapon may still be loaded."

John may not have known anything about guns, but he wasn't stupid. He had been thinking of little else. "Right here," he replied, pointing at the rear of the barrel where it showed through the large, mostly rectangular hole in the top of the gun.

Kitch nodded. "The chamber. Keep holding the gun in your right hand—finger off the trigger. Now with the thumb and forefinger of your left hand, grab the rear of the slide—the top of the pistol that goes back and forth—and pull it back. It's hard at first, but after the first time your muscles learn the task, you'll wonder why you ever thought so. That's right, now peek through the ejection port—the big rectangular hole—into the chamber. See a cartridge?"

"No. No cartridge in the chamber."

"Okay, try to remember always to check the gun in that order, magazine first, chamber second. Otherwise—"

"Otherwise, I could be checking what starts out to be an empty chamber, but if there's a cartridge in the magazine, I could be loading it just by moving the slide back far enough to look, right?"

"You're a good student, John, but we knew that, didn't we?"

"Thank you, Professor Sinclair, you're right. My grade-point was always higher than yours."

"But the girls always liked me better, and what else is college for? Now the scary part: first, put these ear protectors on. You can still hear pretty well, these things are for stopping really *loud* noises. Now take these safety glasses. Since I wear glasses all the time, I'll stick with what I've got. All set?"

"Think so. What do I do now?"

"Dry-fire—shoot the gun without ammo—until you know what you're doing. Hold it in your right hand. Lay your index finger on the side of the trigger guard, rather than the trigger. Wrap your left hand around the right, left index below the trigger guard. Now extend your arms and lock your elbows. That's the "isosceles" position, if you recall your junior high geometry. Squeeze—the handle, not the trigger—until your hands just start to tremble, then back the pressure off until the trembling just stops. That's how hard you're supposed to hold the gun. It'll come automatically with enough practice. Peek, and you'll see the grip-checkering embossed on your right palm."

So it was. But it didn't seem to hurt. "Now what?"

"With your left thumb—leave your hands where they are—cock the hammer. Right, all the way back until it locks. Now look at the top of the weapon, at the sights. Center the front sight between the ears of the rear sight, with all three elements at the same level. Now, keeping the sights in that position, move the gun until the target down there seems to sit atop the front sight like an apple on a post. Focus on it—let the rear sight and the target be blurry, but keep the front sight sharp."

It took John several tries to follow all of those directions at once. He'd taken tennis lessons that were like this.

"Now, gently, put your finger on the trigger and slowly increase the pressure until—nope! You jerked it. I saw the muzzle bob. The bullet would have hit three feet low. The idea is to have the sights in the same position, centered, level, right beneath the target *after* you've pulled the trigger as it was before. Try again."

John practiced the motions over and over again until Kitch was satisfied he was doing it all right, and all at the same time. He learned to take a deep breath and let half of it out before he pulled the trigger, and he learned what seemed very unnatural to him, to let the target remain a blur and keep the front sight in focus.

Finally, it was time for the real thing. By now, several other shooters had shown up and taken their places on the line, and he was grateful for the ear ptotectors. He couldn't see what kind of guns they were making all the noise with; he was trying to concentrate on his father's .45. Carefully following Kitch's instructions, he took the first step toward actually shooting a real gun.

"Put the magazine into the pistol—keep it pointed downrange! Now pull the slide all the way back and release it. Keep your finger off the trigger. That's right. Now you have a live cartridge in the chamber. Aim the piece the way you did before— keep that bullseye on top the front sight—and *squeeze* the trigger."

John did as instructed. His father's .45 bucked in his hand and roared as it went off. He blinked, then looked 50 feet down range to where Kitch had hung a paper target on something resembling a clothes line and sent it halfway downrange using an electric-powered pully system. Even from here, he could see a gaping half-inch hole he'd put in the paper, a handspan below and to the left of the target's center.

Meanwhile, the pistol had prepared itself for the next shot, cocking the hammer, ejecting the empty case, and chambering a new one. This time, knowing what to expect, he held it steadier. This time, the recoil almost felt good and he could smell the powder smoke in the air. This time, and the next three times, the huge bullet holes seemed to march closer and closer to the center. The last two hit exactly in the center, overlapping like cloverleaves.

God help me, he thought, as the slide locked back on an emptied magazine, I have a natural talent for this!

And in that instant, the venerable 1911A1 ceased to be his father's and became his.

CHAPTER SEVENTEEN:
DIVINE JULIUS

Until this moment, the whole thing had been a blur, scented with hundreds of burning beeswax candles and the smell of evergreen from the holiday altar dressings and a huge Christmas tree at the back of the church.

John's snow-white holiday vestments, garments he'd worn more than half a lifetime, seemed alien to him this afternoon, like a Halloween costume. They were supposed to be little more than the everyday clothing worn by ancient Romans. The streets of Rome, he reflected, not for the first time, must have looked very strange with thousands of priests wandering their cattle-pathway lengths, and no civilians.

Beneath almost everything else, he wore an amice, the "helmet of Salvation", meaning trust in Jesus Christ, a white linen cloth that covered his neck and shoulders, not unlike a fringed Jewish prayer shawl. It smelled a little of the mothballs it had been kept in for a year, an odor he unconsciously associated with holidays,

Over that, he wore the alb, a long white linen "nightgown" meant to symbolize the purity of soul a priest should possess to ascend to the altar. It always made him feel guilty to put it on, but then Catholic guilt was universally infamous, ubiquitous, and fully dense enough to be chainsawed into huge blocks to build cathedrals with.

About his waist he wore the cincture, a white tassled cord (what was it with religions and tassles, anyway?) that was also emblematic of priestly purity, and over his left forearm, like a wine steward's towel, he'd placed the maniple. He'd never quite figured that one out. What part of ancient Roman clothing did that represent? Was it a sort of atrophied version of the long train of a toga you always saw draped over a Roman senator's forearm in the movies? He'd never dared to ask the sisters in school, and by the time he was attending the seminary, he was so accustomed to it, he'd forgotten to ask.

Over the alb he wore the stole, its ends crossed over the breast, another sort of shawl symbolizing the spiritual powers and dignity (what he felt of them) of a priest. Over all that came the chasuble, a garment like the three musketeers wore in the movies.

On this doubly special occasion—Christmas Day and the young priest's final duties at St. Gabriel's—Father Joseph acted as his Server, a responsibility usually laid upon one of the acolytes. It had been an unusual request, but John had granted it gladly, seeing in it a renewed faith and rededication on Joseph's part that he sincerely wished he felt himself. Together they performed the ancient ritual in preparation for the Mass and exchanged the sacred words.

"Emitte lucem tuam et veritatem tuam," John intoned the familar words. "Send forth Your light and

Your fidelity. *Ipsa me deduxerunt et adduxerunt in montem sanctum tuum, et in tabernacula tua.* They shall lead me on and bring me to Your holy mountain and to your dwelling-place."

Joseph responded brightly, clearly finding new meaning in the old words, *"Et introibo ad altare Dei: ad Deum qui laetificat juventutem meam.* Then I will go into the altar of God, the God of my gladness and joy."

So it was, through another Antiphon, through the Confiteor *(Mea culpa, mea culpa, mea maxima culpa!)*, to the Introit, the Kyrie, and the Gloria. Knowing what was coming, the only Latin that seemed truly appropriate to John was what Julius Caesar had said when, violating Roman law and custom, he'd taken his personal army with him across the Rubicon, into Italy: *"Alia jacta est:* the die is cast."

Following the appropriate prayer and the Epistle for the day, Gallatians 4:1-7, and a psalm that ended, "My heart overflows with a goodly theme; as I sing my ode to the King, my tongue is nimble as the pen of a skillful scribe," (one can only hope, he thought), came the Gospel, Luke 2:33-40: "And Simeon blessed them and said to Mary His Mother, 'Behold, this Child is destined for the fall and for the rise of many in Israel, and for a sign that shall be contradicted.'" He'd always wondered about that passage. Now it seemed strangely fitting.

He scarcely noticed the offertory, so used was he to the ritual, so preoccupied with what he would do next. Finally, the wait was over and he addressed a congregation swollen (as it would be at Easter) by a holiday few Catholics failed to acknowledge by attending church. Inhaling deeply and noticing again the sweet scent of candles and the sharp, bracing aroma of evergreen, he leaned over the pulpit.

"On this holiest, most awesome, and joyful of all the days in the Christian calendar, I come before you to speak—not out of any temporal or spiritual authority that, together, we might imagine I possess—but simply as another human being who, having reached a branching of the road in the journey of his life, peers intently (and not without some anxiety) at whatever maps he's been given, trying to find the way.

"Recently, it would be fair to say that my life had followed an entirely different course than the path I see before me now. To fall upon another metaphor, you might say that my existence has been turned upside down. I belabor you with some of the facts only to show you the kind of jolt that we must take sometimes in order to bring us back to an awareness of who we really are, and what God demands of us.

"As many of you know, my father, Ed Greenwood, was killed not long ago. Ordinarily—especially in such a setting as this—we might agree to the phrase, 'he passed away'. But reality demands that the premature and absolutely purposeless end of my father's kind, wise, and productive life be described as it happened: he was nothing more than a randomly selected victim, viciously put to death by barbarians and looters, for whatever cash he happened to have in his pockets. Please remember that, because it becomes important later on.

"Only a day or two previously, I had learned—although at first, of course, I wanted desperately to deny it—that Ed Greenwood was not, in fact, my father. Nor was Julia Greenwood," he nodded at her where she was sitting down near the front, "that beloved, dear woman with whom many of you are well acquainted, truly my mother. Who they were ... well, half a century ago, they were generous strangers who saved a little boy from being kidnapped and murdered by the same kind of subhumans—and by that I mean those who chose to relinquish their humanity to become mindless predators—who murdered the man I believed was my father.

"Ed and Julia Greenwood were not my parents, nor was I even myself, John Greenwood, but Abram Herschel Rosen, orphaned son of David and Etta Rosen who, like Ed Greenwood, fell victim to criminal butchers. To put it succinctly, I am a Jewish Holocaust orphan given a second chance to live by good, decent, God-fearing Christians. Because of their love of Christ and for the Jewish people, I am alive today.

"Naturally, this new and initially unwelcome knowledge engendered many uncertainties and changing attitudes toward myself, my faith, and, surprisingly, toward the nature of the relationship between individuals and the government. Along the way, I discovered three things I should have known all along but chose to overlook or deny.

"First, it doesn't matter whether criminal butchers lurk in dark, dangerous inner city streets, hold lying press conferences in tents on the wind-whipped Texas prairie, or strut forth in well-tailored suits and uniforms, on high platforms, in broad daylight, adored by drooling millions—they're *still* criminal butchers, cut from the same cloth.

"Second, the appropriate response to criminal butchers is not meekly to offer them your throat, however well-meaningly I've misled you to do so all these years. I was wrong; I apologize and beg your forgiveness. Joel 3:10 tells us, 'Beat your plowshares into swords and your pruninghooks into spears: let the weak say I am strong.' And Jesus himself said that if you have no sword, you should sell your robe, if you must, and buy one.

"Third, it is equally inappropriate to seek protection from criminal butchers by rushing to embrace yet another gang of criminal butchers.

"Now on one hand, you might say this is nothing but common sense. The Lord never asked us to be helpless, indeed, history has shown that He is most inclined to help those who help themselves. Certainly He helped the partisans among my newly-discovered family who helped themselves against the Nazis. On the other hand, you might say this is only philosophy. What does it mean? What does it mean to me? What practical connection does it have with my everyday life?

"For the past several weeks, I've spent a great deal of time with people for whom it means everything. In living memory, their fathers and mothers, sisters and brothers, sons and daughters, husbands and wives, friends and neighbors were rounded up by the criminal butchers I mentioned—criminal *government* butchers—and taken away to meet a fate so horrible that any truly deep contemplation of it would sicken the firmest constitution and drive strong men and women insane.

"Some of them, like some of us, believe that the way to deal with this is to pretend it can never happen again, although they live in one of America's most crime-ridden cities, in a nation where 82 men, women, and children—two dozen beautiful little children—were confined, tortured, gassed, shot, and burned to death in their church by their own government, on a planet drenched in innocent blood from pole to pole. Implicitly or explicitly, they think the best way is to be passive, to do nothing, to deny the unpleasant responsibility we all have for preserving our own lives and those of our loved ones. They think thereby perhaps to avoid being noticed by the criminal butchers around us.

"Of them I would ask, when criminal butchers strike and reality imposes itself upon you—while your friends and neighbors who want to remain able to evade acknowledging reality look away— why is your first impulse to throw yourself into the arms of a government that doesn't care whether you live or die, wouldn't help you to survive if it could, and is historically far likelier to turn on you and tear you to pieces itself at the least encouragement?

"It is vital that you know that in court case after court case, the government—federal, state, and local—which claims to protect you and takes half of what you earn to pay for it, absolutely denies responsibility for your safety. And at the same time, in places like Chicago and New York, it forbids you the means to defend yourself unless, in some 'enlightened' jurisdictions, you come and beg for its permission to defend your own life.

"The evil, cowardly, and corrupt politicians who created this insane contradiction are eager to impose it, not just on Chicago and New York, but on the rest of the country, as well. They even copied their gun laws from the Nazis! Just consider what happened at Mount Carmel, near Waco, Texas. Nor are they content to stop at that. They wish to render every individual in the world defenseless against criminal butchers, and their principle instrument in fulfilling that wish is the United Nations.

"Watch the news: the UN works to disarm whole populations exactly the same way the Nazis did, rendering them as vulnerable to genocide as the Jews in 1930s' Germany. Don't think for a minute that they mean to exclude America. They don't, and they will tell you so, openly. Waco was only the beginning.

"A moment ago I pretended to hear you ask, 'What does all this mean to me? What practical connection does it have with my everyday life?' For myself, I can tell you that I can no longer work at the task I've been assigned by the diocese, to help prepare the city for United Nations Appreciation Week. Given what I've learned, it would be too much like helping to prepare for 'Genocide Appreciation Week'.

"Nor can I take part in honoring the ambassador of Japan, a nation that kidnapped thousands of women during World War II and sterilized them to serve as unwilling 'comfort' for its troops, a nation that looted and burned its way across Asia stopping only to seize babies by the ankles and splatter their brains out against walls, a nation that let its soldiers *eat* prisoners of war, a nation that now denies these acts that millions witnessed, a nation that still tortures confessions out of suspects and searches its subjects' houses on a regular basis for drugs, guns, or whatever else it disapproves of—and feels it can use the UN to condemn America because some us remain free to own and carry the means of defending ourselves against exactly such atrocies as that barbaric nation is unrepentant of.

"They're all the same, criminal butchers, whether they're muggers in a Chicago alley, baby-killers on the Llano Estacado, or the rapists of Nanking. Of *course* they want us disarmed. Of *course* they want us helpless. Ultimately, they mean to seize everything we've earned, everything we love, and make us their slaves or kill us. Probably the worst thing about this latest gang of criminal butchers is that they want to replace our Bill of Rights with the empty promises of the so-called 'United Nations Universal Declaration of Human Rights'.

"While the Delaration of Human Rights pretends to secure many of the rights Americans are accustomed to, it's a cruel hoax. Unlike the Bill of Rights, it guarantees nothing. It omits many of our rights—those guaranteed by the Tenth, Ninth, Eighth, Seventh, Sixth, Fifth, Fourth, Third, Second, and First Amendment. It makes them all subject to approval by the very governments most likely to suppress them. It forbids action on the part of people—like the American Revolution—to secure their rights. It forcibly imposes a perpetual tax-and-spend welfare state on every productive individual anywhere in the world. And finally, in Article 29, it says, 'These rights and freedoms'—meaning the power of the one-world government to impose itself on us—'may in no case be exercised contrary to the purposes and principles of the United Nations'.

"In short, it would accomplish what neither Hitler nor Stalin was able to do, destroy individual human liberty for all time, and make us all slaves of the state. It would impose on us a revolutionary socialist regime without firing a shot.

"To quote writer Richard Stevens, whose analysis of the United Nations I found on the internet, 'Everyone must clearly understand that the Universal Declaration, and the one-world government that proclaims it, are the enemies of the American vision of government and liberty.

Americans must reject the Universal Declaration, and enthusiastically celebrate and protect their precious Bill of Rights.'

"I'll go a step further. With just as much legitimate authority as the UN had to make it in the first place—and resting all of my worldly faith, hope, and trust in the Declaration of Independence and the highest law of the land, the 'Bill of Rights'—as an American, I hereby declare *their* deceptive and evil declaration null and void."

CHAPTER EIGHTEEN: BISHOP JARVIS CAMELLE

The phone book *slammed* onto the desktop, causing the phone to bounce. John remembered that in some countries phone books were used as bludgeons during interrogations.

"Exactly what the hell didja think y'were accomplishin' wit' yo' Christmas sermon, Monsignor Greenwood—or should Ah say 'Monsignor *Rosen*?'"

Apparently there had been a tattletale among his congregation yesterday. John had expected that and been prepared for it. But he wondered why he'd never noticed before just how *evil* Bishop Jarvis Camelle looked. The proverb said never judge a book by its cover, but by his age (which John judged to be 10 years younger than himself), the bishop's character had had plenty of time to stamp itself on his outward appearance.

Camelle had a head like a reptile, slickly bald from forehead to as far back as John could see, streamlined from a jutting jaw, set with small, irregular teeth, to the conical back of his skull, as shiny as if he polished it every day. In some ways he resembled a goalie's mask and helmet. A close-cropped fringe rose as far as his back-slanting ears. His eyes were the merest slits, set diagonally, glittering cruelly as he spoke in his peculiar southern accent. John had heard that the bishop was originally from Louisiana. Wherever he was from, when he said "world" or "girl", it came out "woild" or "goil" just as clearly as if he'd hailed from Brooklyn.

In his plain, black, floor-length cassock, Camelle looked like something out of a vampire movie. The man could not sit still. Just now, they were in his downtown office, to which John had been summoned peremptorily earlier this morning, a room large enough, he thought, to play hockey in, if the floor had been covered with ice instead of carpet worth hundreds of dollars per square yard. Equally expensive-looking heavy velvet draperies along two walls of the corner office shut out the morning sun. The desk looked almost like the flight deck of a nuclear-powered aircraft carrier—there was nothing on its glass top but the directory he'd thrown there and the telephone—and the chair behind it like a throne. Yet Camelle paced back and forth in front of his desk—John was surprised to see that there wasn't noticeable wear to the carpet—as rapidly as if he were running a footrace, waving his arms wildly, and throwing his head from side to side.

"Sir," John offered, "I was only telling the truth as I—"

"What truth, son?" Camelle demanded, as if he were older than John and his father or a coach. He stopped pacing and leaned over to shake a finger at John. "Theah's an infinite numbah of truths. Yo' truth, mah truth, ever'body else's truth. The Lawd's truth an' the devil's truth. The truth's jus' purely plain subjective, son, an' consensual. It's yo' job t'tell a *responsible* truth we-all can agree on!"

John spread his hands in a helpless gesture. "But St. Thomas Aquinas—"

"*Stuff* St. Thomas Aquinas! We-all have an obligation t'one anothah in this vale of misery, an' in any diocese Ah'm runnin', that don't include preachin' no right-wing militia subversive gobbledegook! It was one thing, John, when you were a disciple of ... what was her name? Dorothy Day. Thomas Merton. Theah's precedent f'that, it goes along wit' the program. Once ever'body agrees wit' her, s'gonna be a peaceful, kindly, orderly, an' easily-managed woild."

Camelle resumed pacing. "A man can discover any amounta truth, son, but if it leads to undesirable results, then it's best set aside in favor of some othah truth that helps get us t'where we want t'go."

"I don't think I follow you, sir." A small lie. He knew exactly where the man was headed. He'd led so many others there, himself.

"Ah know y'don't, son, but Ah'll help ya. Take this gun thing. B'lieve me, as one of the fo'most gun control advocates in America, somewhere right between Charlie Schumer an' Sarah Brady, Ah *know* the stats where guns are concerned. B'tween you an' me, here in mah sanctum sanctorum, fo' every life they take, they probbly save a hundred. Fact is, Ah keep a .357 in the top drawer of this heah desk, an' mah security men all carry high capacity semi-automatic pistols."

John wondered if the bishop's revolver was

licensed. He played golf once a week with the mayor, and this was Chicago, after all, so it almost certainly was. In perpetuity.

"But what'd happen if *ever'body* knew that particulah truth, son? They'd all go out an' get themselves a gun! An' then where would we be? Ah've seen it befo', back home down south. They'd get t'thinking independently. They'd start believin' they'ah competent t'run their own lives. Then what would you an' Ah an' the mayor an' the governor an' the President do? What excuse would we have for ouah existence?"

John was open-mouthed with outrage. He'd understood Camelle to be a cynical politician who really believed nothing, but he hadn't known it went this far. "Are you saying that, if United Nations troops commit atrocities—don't interrupt me, sir, you started this—looting, rape, and murder in countries where they're supposed to be peace-keepers, that truth should be swept under the rug in the name of some greater good we imagine the UN might do someday?"

The bishop failed to reply for what seemed an eternity. Although John recognized it as a tactic of intimidation, it was effective.

"Lookie heah, son," the bishop's face was screwed up like a wrung washcloth, features drawn into the center. He tilted his head, peering through one squinted eye. "Don't let's us bandy words."

"Is that what we were doing?"

Camelle ignored the question. Walking around his desk to sit in his huge swivel chair, he steepled his fingers. "John, we gonna give you the benefit of the doubt. We gonna assume you'ah distraught by the unfortunate death of youah daddy an' put you on administrative leave a coupla months. Get the hell outa town, son, take a sabbatical. You'll come t'yo senses right enough. Then, when you get back we'll see if we cain't fix you up wit' a little more glamorous assignment. Ah heah there's gonna an openin' for an aide to the archbishop."

"And if I don't come to my senses?"

"Well then, we gonna hafta consider some alternative measures."

"I see." John arose. "Very well, a sabbatical it will be." He was surprised how easy it was to obey this order. He took his coat and hat and, with his hand on the knob of the bishop's office door, turned for a last look at the man. "I'll see you, sir, in two months."

The bishop nodded without saying anything, but once John had left, he picked up the phone. "Mary," he told his secretary, "get me ouah ol' friend Reinie Galen Juniah down t'the Federal Bureau of Investigation."

When they came, they didn't look at all like Mulder and Scully.

In the first place, both of them were male, and rather than slight of stature, they were enormous, even to John, who was a big man himself. Despite their well-tailored suits, they looked as thuggish as any professional hockey player he'd ever seen.

Eleanor had scurried nervously into John's

office, where he sorted papers, preparing for a long absence. Somebody else would have to finish the UN Appreciation Week paperwork. In the light of everything he knew now about that organization, that suited John perfectly.

"Two men are here to see you, Monsignor," she said breathlessly. "They showed me ID cards and said they're from the FBI!"

There had been a time, John thought, when to a person of Eleanor's age and place, a visit from the FBI would have been interesting or exciting, rather than terrifying. What had America become that an innocent and productive human being was afraid of such an event?

He said, "Please show them in, Eleanor."

As she turned to follow his instruction, they were in the room, brushing past as if she weren't there. They both pulled wallets (or whatever they were called) from their jacket pockets and flashed them at John, replacing them before he could make anything of them.

"John Greenwood, alias Johann Gruenwald, alias Abram Herschel Rosen?" one of them demanded. "We're Special Agent Galen and Special Agent Fuhre. We'd like to ask you some questions if you don't mind."

"Or even if I do?" John didn't smile, nor did he rise to greet his "guests" or offer them chairs. He'd had experience with this type in his antiwar days (back then they'd been called the "Federal Bureau of Intimidation") and knew he had no obligation to do anything they demanded. "That's *Monsignor*

Greenwood, by the way. Nor are those other names aliases. If you suggest they are again, you're going to wind up conversing with my lawyer. I was adopted—as I'm sure you know perfectly well—Rosen was my birth name and Gruenwald was my foster parents' name before they anglicized it."

The two men towering over him didn't change their expressions. One said, "Beg your pardon, Monsignor. Agent Fuhre and I have one or two questions we'd appreciate your answering. May we sit down?"

"Only if you're polite." Without being aware of it, John had shifted to hockey coach mode—and suddenly realized that he wouldn't be coaching hockey, possibly for the rest of his life. Doing his best to hide his pain and dismay, he indicated the chairs and nodded.

One of the men—Galen—took out a notebook. "We're here from the Bureau's Chicago office, Monsignor. We happened to hear about the, well, rather unusual sermon you gave yesterday. I don't want you to get the wrong idea about what we're doing here—I can see you already have to some extent—but these are dangerous times we're living through, and we're paid to be alert to threats."

John shook his head. "Threats?"

"To national security. To everybody's health and safety. There are bad people out there who hate America and represent a danger. We keep track of them as best we can, so we wanted to ask who you've been talking to, with regard to what you had to say on Sunday."

John had lived through McCarthy, Johnson, and Nixon, but he could hardly believe what he was hearing. The FBI was investigating an official of the Catholic church because of a sermon? He composed himself. "Let me get this straight: you wish to approve my exercise of religious freedom and free speech, both at the same time? Just what part of the First Amendment don't you gentlemen understand?"

"Don't look at it that way, Monsignor," Galen almost pleaded. "We don't. Our job is protecting America. We have a legitimate need to know who you've been talking to, what web sites you've been looking at, what militia units or terrorists you may have heard about—or if you have knowlege of future plans for political violence in America."

"From the internet, or from the confessional?" It was all John could do to keep from hissing it through his teeth. Rigid with anger, he looked from one of the agents to the other and said, "Everything I spoke of yesterday can be found, if you care to look, in places like the *World Almanac & Book of Facts*—that includes the United States Constitution which says in plain English that my right to deliver any sermon I like is protected by the highest law of the land."

Galen shook his head, as if addressing a small, recalcitrant little boy. "I'm afraid that the Constitution may have to be set aside in the near future, Monsignor, for the good of the country. Terrorism is a clear and present danger. Americans will just have to get used to losing some of the freedoms that they've been privileged to have in the past, in order to fight it."

"What you mean, Special Agent Galen, is that the Cold War, which was phony to begin with, is regrettably over, and that you now need a new excuse to keep us under your thumb and tax us half to death."

For the first time the other agent, Fuhre, opened his mouth to speak, the expression on his face nothing short of murderous. Galen reached out to silence him, and started to say something, himself.

John preempted him. "I agree with you that terrorism is a clear and present danger—but the only group guilty of it in America is the US government, at places like Ruby Ridge and Waco."

Fuhre was white-lipped with anger, not about to be silenced by his partner. He stood, fists clenched. "For your information, I was *at* Waco! Every law enforcement officer there acted properly and with valor! The FBI never fired a single shot! And in any case, FBI procedures are none of your— or anybody else's—business!"

"Unless this happened to be a democracy or something." John rose to meet his eyes. "Never fired a shot? Except for your so-called Hostage Rescue Team and their friends out back with machineguns and Ferret missiles. By the way, what ever happened to *peace* officers? Go peddle it somewhere else, Special Agent Fuhre, nobody's buying it here."

On his feet, Galen finally got his partner under

control. "You'll hear from us again, count on it."

Fuhre added, "Don't tell anyone we were here!"

CHAPTER NINETEEN: ROBERT HEINLEIN

Somehow, John had expected it to be different.

He supposed what he'd unconsciously expected was to emerge from the TWA airliner into the broiling Mediterranean desert sun, onto one of those self-propelled stairways they used to wheel up to airplanes so passengers could hoof it across half a mile of heat-shimmering asphalt or concrete to the terminal.

That wasn't the way at Ben-Gurion International Airport, in beautiful downtown Lod, on the outskirts of Tel Aviv. In the first place, it was only 65 degrees (his estimate, doing calculations in his head from a measuring system people might have liked less if they knew it had been decreed by Napoleon, the Hitler of the 19th century), and from what few glimpses he'd had, the sky was overcast.

He understood from guidebooks that he wouldn't see the sky directly, or feel a breeze on his face, for at least an hour and a half, and only if his passport and other documents passed muster and one of the thousand soldiers that surrounded him everywhere didn't hiccup and spray him down with submachinegun bullets. He'd hoped (corruptly, he admitted), that in a land where religion was a major industry, his collar might speed things along. It may, in fact, have made him look more like a suspicious character. The thing to wear, it seemed, was a pair of khaki shorts and a Hawaiian shirt.

And whatever hat came to hand, the dumber-looking the better.

John loved airports, even the smell of kerosene, if it weren't for the "security" procedures that made them all seem like a little piece of Bulgaria. There was no good reason for it. A suitably equipped populace, he now understood, was the best guarantee of social order. How had Robert Heinlein put it? "An armed society is a polite society." But governments would rather handle people like live-stock and were willing to tolerate the occasional (and inevitable) bloody failure of their hired guns, if it meant they could keep their subjects helpless.

Intelligently, he'd only brought one small check-through and a smaller carry-on. He hadn't even brought a camera; he wasn't here in Israel to take pictures, he was here to see. And those, he'd learned the hard way over many years, were two very different processes.

The last hurdle he cleared was customs. He looked at his watch (taking in with it, the mush-room-shaped birthmark that had gotten him into all this) and saw that exactly 93 minutes had elapsed since he'd walked through the elevated cattle-chute from the 747 into the terminal, achiev-ing an objective—stepping over an imaginary line on a map—that in a free world would have taken less than a second. (That, he realized, was the cost of keeping a 20th century super-state: human progress slowed by a factor of five thousand.) Apparently they weren't interested in his shirts, clean underwear, and extra pair of walking shoes. They passed him through and turned their attentions on a dangerous-looking little old lady with a walker.

Once outside the terminal with both bags, he turned right, as he'd been instructed in Chicago by someone who'd made this trip several times. There he found the "sherut", a Mercedes van not unlike one that had picked him up at St. Gabriel's and taken him to O'Hare. It was more expensive than the airport bus—36 New Israeli shekels, or about 10 dollars—but it would take him exactly where he wanted to go, a moderately-priced Days Inn in Jerusalem, about 45 minutes away.

In some ways, it was a small world, after all. The driver wore a cap with a tiny cloisonne pin of Marvin the Martian. Once safely in his seat—as far back as he could manage on the right hand side— John could lean back, relax, and think about the reasons he was here in a way he hadn't been able to manage on the nine-hour flight.

The "someone who'd made this trip several times" was Kitch Sinclair. Kitch was one of those mysterious individuals who'd been everywhere and done everything (he'd even visited Antarctica where he'd been photographed with penguins and invited by the "locals" to ski down the side of an active volcano) and yet always seemed to be in whenever a friend called. John often accused him of being twins.

"Clones," Kitch corrected him after the most

recent accusation. "There are at least six of us—or seven, I lose count sometimes. But that's hardly important now, seeing as how you've been fired".

"Not fired, suspended." John shook his head. They were in his friend's home, a small, freestanding stone carriage house in one of the older neighborhoods. He'd inherited it from his parents and paid for it several times over since then in property taxes. But it had ivy growing up two sides, a serpentine flagstone walk, mullioned bay windows with arches at the tops, two stories, a finished basement, and a finished attic where Kitch had built a *camera obscura*, a sort of periscope for looking out over the city housetops on a rare, occasional clear day.

They sat there now, in big reclining chairs, looking down into a shallow bowl, painted reflective white, where the outdoor images were cast. John drank coffee. Kitch had one of the sixpack of New Belgium Fat Tire John had brought him from Colorado and then forgotten about. Tidying up, he'd discovered it at the back of the refrigerator.

"Suspended until you recant, Galileo, if I get the bishop's drift. Are you going back after two months to tell him you were wrong and he's right about the UN and everything else? If you plan to, I want to know what you did with my best friend John, you alien imposter!"

Kitch *was* his best friend, for all that he was an atheist and, as far as John knew, an anarchist, too. What did he call himself? Libertarian. John wondered if he voted that way. Or bothered to vote at all. But who else could be trusted to have Nestle Quik for his coffee—and be there when disaster had befallen him?

John took another sip of coffee, wishing for a cigarette. "No, I won't recant. I don't have any idea what I'm going to do. I can't perform Mass. I can't even coach hockey any more. Believe me, that hurts!"

"I'll bet!" Kitch laughed. "The Scouts'd probably let you coach. Too bad the seminary—say, what're you going to do for money?"'

John shrugged. "I'm still on salary. Once two months are up, I don't know. I've never made much, but I've never spent much, either. And in the 23 years I've been at St. Gabriel's, I've never taken a vacation. I have some money set aside, and I inherited some from my father. And it isn't as if I had rent to pay."

"I'll bet Camelle doesn't want to get sued. What he did is actionable, you know. The Pope himself can't order you to have some given political opinion. Any decent lawyer would make hash of him in court. And didn't he start your confrontation off with an anti-Semitic remark?"

John grinned. "He called me Monsignor Rosen—that's who I am: Monsignor Abram Herschel Rosen! Hardly interpretable as anti-Semitic, even if I were inclined to sue. But we're not speaking of my welfare, here. We're speaking of the church I've served for 30 years. It wouldn't be helping to sue it."

Some picture in Kitch's mind caused him to

grin right back. "Even if it put a metaphorical plastic bag around the church and fumigated amoral vermin like Camelle in the process? Maybe they'll let you transfer—you could be *Rabbi* Rosen."

"I've thought of that. But a man has to know who he is before he can decide what he's going to be. Kitch, I don't know who I am! I'm Jewish! My mom's my stepmother! I have lustful thoughts about my high school girlfriend—there, I said it and I'm glad! And I own a gun! Hell, everybody I *know* owns a gun!"

"Lustful thoughts about Sheila?" Kitch's eyebrows did a jig over his eyes. "When did this happen?"

John sighed and put his face in his hands. Suddenly the attic seemed stuffy and he longed for the clear, cool air of the rink from which he felt exiled. "About the time I learned she was getting a divorce—and that rabbis are usually married."

"That's the healthiest development I've heard in four decades. Does she know you're having lustful thoughts? If I remember Sheila, she'd be flattered but not surprised."

"Kitch!" John was genuinely shocked. "How can I think when you talk like that? My options don't include surrendering myself to temptations of the flesh!"

"How quaintly put," Kitch was unabashed. "Someday, remember I said you couldn't be more wrong. She's loved you for a lifetime. She used to hang around the college hoping you'd change your mind. But you never did, poor fool."

"If romance is all that great, how come you never married?"

Kitch shrugged, attempting to make a small thing of it. "Because while she was pining away for you, I fell in love with her."

The two old friends talked late into the night. After Kitch's surprising confession, which didn't bear too much discussion anyway, they managed to shift the conversation to politics, which was what John had wanted to talk about. It dismayed him that he seemed to be joining a side that dipped snuff, listened to whiney, nasal music, and carried rifles in the back windows of their pickups.

Kitch agreed with most of what John had learned from Asher and Albert or found on the internet about the UN, the racist roots of "victim disarmament", and a hundred other issues established "wisdom" saw differently. What puzzled John was that, while they got their views, ultimately, from their religion, Kitch was an atheist. "So how come you agree with these two old Jews and conservatives like my dad, not to mention Mike Reagan, Alan Keyes, and Gordon Liddy?"

He was anxious to know the answer; he thought it might be the key to everything. They were down in the kitchen now, having taken delivery of several foam plastic boxes of Mexican food. Inside were chips and a bowl of hot, sweet, liquid cheese, beef and bean burritos smothered in green chili, pork and avacado tacos. (How would he live with the dietary rules if he decided to be Jewish;

half the food he loved most was forbidden!)

"I suppose they'd say a broken clock is right twice a day," Kitch replied, sipping a margarita. "We don't agree on everything. Ask me about abortion. What I believe, John, is that I'm the owner of my life and all the products of my life. That can be derived from first principles, just like plane geometry, if you've got a couple hours. The political side is that respect for universal self-ownership means that nobody has a right to trespass on anybody else's property. Since the only practical way you can do that is by force or threat of force, libertarians forbid its initiation."

John blinked. "Its initiation?"

"Nobody's allowed to start it. If they do, they've bought into a world of grief." He patted his right hip. John knew that under his sweater he carried a small but powerful pistol, a Star FireStar, in a caliber he'd never known existed, .40 Smith & Wesson. A second reason he'd come tonight was that, not knowing where he was going to live for two months, he wanted to leave his .45 with Kitch. At the moment it was still up in the attic in its zippered leather pouch.

"This is Ayn Rand stuff, right?"

Kitch replied, "There are many contributors to the philosophy: Robert LeFevre, Leonard Reed, Henry Hazlitt, 19th century thinkers like Lysander Spooner and Benjamin Tucker."

"And can it tell me what I should do now?"

Kitch tipped his chair back. "Well, you could light a cigarette.

You've been brave all evening, John, but you're driving me crazy."

John took out his box of Shermans, lit one, and inhaled. "You're evading the issue, Kitch."

"Not at all. Say you accept the idea that you own yourself. Maybe the best idea is a sort of personal real-estate appraisal. You know what you've been most of your life. You've just learned what you were when you were very young. Maybe the best thing is to go looking, as the trendy expression has it, for your roots."

"Go to Germany?"

Kitch shook his head. "To Israel."

CHAPTER TWENTY:
OSKAR SCHINDLER

Kitch, of course, had meant his spiritual roots, an interesting conclusion, he thought, for an atheist to reach. Roots, both Jewish and Christian, that were to be found in only one place in the world.

After some deliberation—about 30 seconds' worth—he'd decided to try Kitch's suggestion. Within a week, he'd found himself here in Israel, enjoying an afternoon in which he didn't try to do anything but relax, followed by a long, healthy night's sleep—strategies intended to fend off several thousand miles' worth of jet lag.

The next day, he visited Bethlehem.

From the beginning, back in Chicago, he'd thought about walking the five miles south from Jerusalem to the town of Jesus' birth, a sort of miniature pilgrimage that would have taken at least a couple of hours, past a number of points of minor interest, like the home of the prophet Nathan. But it would have to be with a group, and he was here to contemplate his future alone. He didn't think he could tolerate small-talk with elderly businessmen from a dozen countries and their overweight, badly-dressed wives.

In the end, he took an ordinary tour bus that dropped him off—in a colorful non-clerical short-sleeved shirt, jeans, and Reeboks—along with three dozen other passengers in Manger Square, a name that filled him with misgiving. He'd come for answers, not as a tourist visiting "Jesusland", which was what the place immediately made him think of. In Hebrew, Bethlehem was "Bet Lechem"—"house of bread"; in Arabic, it was "Bet Lahm"—"house of meat". He wondered why there wasn't a McDonald's next door to the Church of the Nativity to celebrate the linguistic coincidence.

Playing tourist for a little while, he got in line to enter the low doorway (built either to keep medieval horse-warriors out or make Christians feel humble in what was Moslem territory at the time) and look over the hideously over-decorated altar. The place was kept by Greek Orthodox priests, Armenians, and Franciscans. Down a pair of narrow stone staircases, he (and half a hundred others) found what was advertised as the grotto of the nativity, and the manger itself, the wall over the cave marked with a simple silver star.

It was an unusually warm day, but he was glad to get back up into the blistering sunlight. The shrine had been built in the fourth century by the mother of Emperor Constantine; there was no reason to believe it was the real place of Jesus' birth. It was far more likely that some canny local peasant back in 326 AD was interested in getting a fat tip from a famous and powerful tourist and identified the place because she seemed to like it. He wondered if there had been quite as many gift shops when the emperor's mom was here.

Then and there he decided not to go to Nazareth. Instead, he returned to Jerusalem and that afternoon, aided by the Frommer's tourist guide that Eleanor had given him as a goodbye present, joined a small group retracing the steps—known as the "Via Dolorosa"—that Jesus had taken to Calvary.

It was a peculiar sensation to be here. John had performed the Stations of the Cross countless times at St. Gabriel's and other churches, as a young member of a Chicago Catholic congregation, later as a seminary student, finally as a priest and then a monsignor. Now John's life, strangely enough, had brought him to the very place it had actually happened. (Unlike Bethlehem, there was some historic support for much of this tradition.) It began with the Sanctuaries of the Flagellation and Condemnation where Jesus was whipped, judgment passed on him, and he had been given the cross to carry.

Some of the paving stones here, it was said, had been trod on by Christ. Listening to the guide's overly-rehearsed commentary and the other tourists chattering away in seven or eight different languages was unnerving to him.

At last they set out along a path that took him and the companions he was trying to ignore from one doorway with semicircular settings of paving stones before it and sculptures over it to another. The custom was to knock and be admitted by a monk or nun. Some prayed, others lectured. More than one tourist listened to pop music on earphones.

At the intersection of the Street of the Valley

(also known as El Wad; everything here had at least two names) and St. Mary's Street, Jesus had fallen for the first time—the third Station of the Cross. In other places he had met his mother, spoken to people, fallen again, or accepted the aid of a kindly stranger, each event becoming part of what was now an ancient ritual.

Finally they arrived at the Church of the Holy Sepulcher—an incomprehensible aggregation of domes, arches, and rooftop platforms, reminiscent of an M.C. Escher drawing—believed to be built atop the mount of Calvary, and taking in Golgotha where Jesus had died, and the tomb in which (however temporarily) he had been interred.

John returned to his hotel feeling strangely unmoved. Perhaps it was because everything had been overbuilt by the idiot Crusaders or by others who had come before or after. He'd always pictured Golgotha outdoors on a stormy day. They'd done their medieval best to turn it into a drive-in. It seemed blasphemous—an excess of organized religion at its worst—to build anything over the site.

Having eaten, he fell into deep but troubled sleep, only to be awakened by the childhood nightmare he'd mistakenly thought he was finally rid of.

The next morning found him back in the Old City at the Western Wall—the *Ha-Kotel Ha-Ma'aravi*—the last remains of King Herod the Great's restoration of Solomon's temple, the holiest of Jewish sites. In this pocket-sized country, he was mere blocks—hundreds of yards—from the Via

Dolorosa where he'd been yesterday.

Now he was on his own, still in non-clerical clothing. He'd even picked up a bright green Fuji disposable cardboard camera at the Day's Inn, hoping to blend in. He had no intention of taking pictures.

What had once been known as the Wailing Wall (due to the way some people prayed at it) was more than six stories high, made of enormous stone blocks called ashlars, some weighing as much as 400 tons. It hadn't been a wall of the Temple, but a retaining wall supporting the hill the Temple had been built on. Above head level, grass grew through the spaces between the blocks, but below, thousands upon thousands of paper prayers had been stuffed into the cracks. John was interested to see that the prayerful were segregated by sex, as he knew they were in Orthodox synagogues back home. He knew that this would never have gone over with Asher's Reform congregation.

He also knew he had to see the 50-foot high hand-hammered copper Scroll of Fire atop the Martyr's Forest, where a tree was planted for each individual—four and a half million pines for adults, a million and a half cedars for children—lost to the Holocaust, called in Hebrew the *Shoah*. The double scroll, which looked rather like a giant torah, pictorially recorded the history of the Jewish people. He had to walk around each scroll, between them, to see it all, all the time smelling pine and cedar that came to him on the breeze.

Used to the Illinois prairies and vast evergreen

forests of the Rockies, John was surprised at how little room six million trees took up. He'd once calculated that the population of the world would fit—standing room only—into Connecticut. It was only the human mind that found the number six million hard to encompass. The enormity of the Holocaust was the worst obstacle to making it real.

Between the Martyr's Forest and the Holocaust memorial of Yad Vashem, lay the Grove of the Righteous, its plantings commemorating heroic and compassionate non-Jews—people like Per Anger and Raoul Wallenberg—who'd risked everything to save victims of Nazi evil. One had been Sempo Sugihara, a Japanese consul in Kovno, Lithuania.

Next came the Hall of Names, a place where millions of pages of information on individual victims were collected, sorted, and stored. With the help of one of the Yad VaShem staff, a girl with curly red hair and green eyes, he found the file on David and Etta Rosen.

Simple words, "found the file". Here were the documents, birth certificates, marriage license. Here were photos similar to those Albert had left with him, different angles, different moments, the same picnic in the country. His hand shook as he looked at papers that were all that remained of two human beings. He stood there for what may have been hours. Then he sat on the floor, back against the cabinets, weeping until the girl—jaded to this sort of grief by her work here—came to tell him it was their time to close.

John couldn't say why he'd been affected that

way. He wasn't certain David and Etta were any more real to him than the day Albert had burst into his office. But they'd been young and happy and in love. And something unspeakably ugly, something that had decided that it owned them and was free to harvest and use them—the same way the ATF and FBI had decided it owned the Branch Davidians—had ended all that forever with the merest negligent flick of an evil hand. However happy his life with Ed and Julia had been, he'd been robbed of another life, the one he'd started with David and Etta.

The final stop on his erratic, self-guided tour was back at the Avenue of the Righteous Among Nations at the final resting place of Oskar Schindler. Like other visitors, he placed another stone atop the grave. He discovered, to his surprise, that he wasn't angry at the Nazis. The appropriate attitude toward them—and more particularly toward the population of tens of millions of "good Germans" who had made their atrocities possible—transcended a little thing like anger. It didn't even belong to the same order of reality.

Six million dead, a million and a half of them children. The ratio was startlingly close to that at Waco. Any government that waged war on children had lost any right to exist. How in the name of God could American Jews have failed to miss the obscenely evil stench of the Holocaust rising from the ashes of Mount Carmel?

No, it was others for whom he felt anger. The Charles Schumers, the Frank Lautenbergs, the

Barney Franks, who violated their solemn oath to uphold and defend the Constitution hundreds of times every day. People like Abraham Foxman, a child Holocaust survivor who now headed the Anti-Defamation League and used it to suppress dissent against the "dominant culture". All the other Jews back home just like them who knew more than he ever would about the *Shoah*, and nevertheless seemed to strive with all their might—and with the help of tens of millions of "good Americans"—to make it all happen again. Could these people be so stupid, so incapable of learning from history, or were they motivated by an inexplicable streak of evil?

Why was it, for example, that they didn't care that Thomas Dodd had cribbed the 1968 Gun Control Act directly from Nazi gun laws?

Worse than all of them, he thought, was the Steven Spielberg crowd of Hollywood writers, director, and producers—the Leni Riefenstahls of the 1990s. Their lies of omission, of facts politically incorrect and inconvenient—for example that the protagonist of *Amistad*, Joseph Cinque, had returned to Africa to become a slaver himself; that Schindler had helped Jews most of all by giving them *guns*—were a crime against their own people and the world.

The night before he'd left, Kitch had told him a story. A famous liberal producer had invited guests into his home. When he'd learned that one of them was interested in guns, he'd showed his guest his own incredibly extensive collection.

"But you're a huge contributor to Handgun Control!" his guest had protested. "Look at these assault rifles, these automatic pistols—they're the very kind of thing you've argued there should be laws against!"

"The laws," the host replied, "are for *them*."

Suddenly, looking down at Schindler's grave, John knew what he must do. He knew who he was, what he was, and what it all meant. He'd heard the cliche about a burden being lifted off one's shoulders. Now he knew what it was all about. He ran down to the taxi that had brought him, lighter on his feet than he'd felt in years.

John returned to the Day's Inn in a serene mood, content and at peace with himself, knowing that he'd come to the right decision. The first thing he did was call to confirm a flight home. He'd had the rather expensive option to return early— although he'd thought he'd never use it—now it was all important to get back.

He looked over the airline schedule. If he packed now and got to Ben-Gurion three hours ahead of time (three hours!) as they demanded, he could take the 10 o'clock flight that would get him home at six AM Jerusalem time, or at one o'clock in the morning, Chicago time.

Anxious to share his happy decision with Kitch, Albert, Sheila, Asher, Julia, Joseph, Eleanor, all those closest to him, he lifted the instrument and punched keys.

"You're listening to the world's largest and most

powerful answering machine ..."

"Kitch, this is John, calling from Jerusalem. You were absolutely right, this *was* the thing to do. My only regret is that what I have to tell you, however earth-shattering, is nothing I want to say over the telephone. I just wanted to thank you for helping me find peace.

"Please tell everyone back there I'll see them when I get home.

"Hell, we can have a party!"

CHAPTER TWENTY-ONE: ALEXIS DE TOCQUEVILLE

It was almost dark outside.

"John has gone to Israel, did you hear?" Albert had just arrived at Asher's home. The two old warriors had been looking forward to this chance to talk for weeks. Asher's wife Helen had set out brandy and home-baked delicacies, then gone downstairs to visit with her grandchildren.

The host smoked his pipe, the guest his strong French cigarettes. Asher was startled at the news about Albert's nephew. He rolled up the top of the foil packet of tobacco and tucked it away in the glass humidor on the small table he kept next to his favorite chair. "I hadn't! What do you suppose got into him?"

"I've no idea," Albert shrugged. He poured brandy from a decanter into the snifter Helen had brought him. He held it up until his salute was answered by his host.

"*Lochaim!*" they both exclaimed, taking a drink.

"I certainly didn't put him up to it," Albert continued. "I wish I had, but he probably wouldn't have listened to me—and I assume you didn't, either. Maybe it was that college professor friend of his, what was his name?"

"Ah, Kitch Sinclair. Dr. Thornton Sinclair. You know, he would have made an excellent rabbi, I think, if it weren't for the slightly inconvenient fact that he's an atheist. Even so, an individual of rare understanding for his age."

Albert laughed. "His age? You're right. Dr. Sinclair's a stripling youth of 50—a mere kid!" Both he and Asher were in their mid-70s.

He took a pull on his unfiltered cigarette, a sip of brandy, and another long pull on his cigarette. He was a man of simple tastes—brandy and cigarettes, cheesburgers and French fries—but he had suffered too much deprivation earlier in his life, and felt there was so little of it left now, that he seized every opportunity to enjoy those simple things that gave him pleasure. The one thing he missed was Rachel, but he'd be seeing her day after tomorrow.

"Never mind that, my friend," he said. "I came to inquire about you. Your congregation, those meshugginahs, have handed you the sack. I saw them do it. What will you do now?"

"Moderately well," Asher raised his eyebrows and puffed on his pipe, filling the room with aromatic smoke. "To paraphrase Benjamin Franklin, those who cherish money more than liberty in the end will have neither. To my immense surprise, and thanks largly to yet another Roman Catholic priest, John's young protege, Father Joseph Spagelli. He telephoned me this morning about my going to work for this new Ralston Foundation that hired him. It seems that he's to be the field man—teaching urban children to defend themselves—and I'm to be the program director."

"Which means?"

"Which means that I will write and speak and act for the Ralston Foundation, write magazine articles and newspaper columns, grant radio and TV interviews, speak at ladies' clubs and business-man's luncheons—on the ethics of self-defense. Also," he rubbed his hands together in gleeful anticipation, "I will fend off the inevitable media and political assaults."

"A perfect job for a rabbi." Albert observed. "Good luck, my friend, you have a long row to hoe. You'll be butting heads with a lot of 'useful idiots'."

"Yes, yes. For me, to rather a large degree, it will consist of rolling back the last hundred years of Jewish history, attempting to untangle the 'fatal embrace' between liberal Jews and socialism. And you're correct, Albert, it will not be easy. I rather imagine my first ladies' club meeting will also be my last, as the word gets around. And liberal Jewish businessmen are so notoriously short-sighted and ... " He hesitated.

"Cowardly?" Albert suggested.

"Well, that might be a little strong." Suddenly his eyes twinkled. "Ah, well, if it were easy, every-body could do it!"

Albert laughed. Nothing could stop this man, could it? "Do you have any idea where you're going to start?" He suddenly noticed that he'd let a long ash grow on his cigarette, a habit he'd always hated and associated with old men. Still listening to Asher, he carefully got the ashtray under the cigarette and flicked the ash off. There. He was young again.

Meanwhile, Asher said, "Yes, Albert, I believe I do. I think we must begin with popularizing the observation that every genocide in history was preceded by gun control—'victim disarmament'. Stalin, Hitler, Mao, Pol Pot. The Turks and the Armenians. The last half century in Africa. Before this, I could say nothing. It would have angered my congregation and ... and cost me my job!"

He laughed heartily. Clearly losing his job had been a price he'd felt he could afford to speak the truth. Albert joined him. "Now what can they do, fire you?"

"How true," Asher replied, "Now all I have to fear is the IRS, the ATF, the FBI, the CIA, the DEA—I don't need to tell you that it's dangerous to be right when the government's wrong. 'Do not ask for whom the black helicopter hovers,'" he misquoted. "That's the first truth we were confronted with as young adults."

Albert nodded but said nothing, remembering. Sometimes his experiences as a partisan were as fresh in his mind as if they'd happened yesterday. So far, at least, his memories of what had happened yesterday were equally clear.

"Joseph will help," Asher mused. "What was that old song about 'Praise the Lord and pass the ammunition'? He's so energetic—already organizing a Bill of Rights Day celebration for next December 15th. The point he'll try to make with this initial observation is that the first 10 amendments to the United States Constitution take precedence over every other law—including the main body of the Constitution itself, and therefore over treaties like the United Nations charter and their phoney-baloney Universal Declaration of Human Rights."

"He thinks he can convey a legal subtlety like that to the general public, given the mass media in this country?" Albert looked skeptical.

"Well if nothing else, it's an elementary exercise in logic, this business about the overriding nature of amendments, but Americans are so poorly educated and so terribly ignorant of their unique political heritage. They don't even seem to know that their rights existed *before* the government did."

Albert shook his head. "It's the public education system that's stripped them of their political senses, dulled them with all of its incessant authoritarian propaganda. Alexis de Tocqueville wouldn't recognize America today as the same nation of ambitious, self-reliant, industrious, literate, self-governing people he visited in 1830 and wrote about. They can't smell or see the evil rising amongst them like a deadly vapor—the War on Drugs, property seizures, cameras everywhere, the Waco massacre, and military live-fire exercise in rural communities. Jews, at least, should know better. You'd think we'd have a better political memory."

Asher agreed. "Not with Judas' goats like Barbra Streisand, Abe Foxman, Wolf Blitzer, Frank Lautenberg, Barney Frank and their ilk to mislead us. And that Spielberg!" He joined Albert in shaking his head until he noticed that they looked like a couple of little plastic dogs in the back window of a car. Setting his brandy snifter down, he got up and looked out the front windows. Although there was no snow falling and the wind was calm, it was as dark and cold outside as a Chicago winter evening could get.

"You know it always amazes me that so many Jews like them still idolize Franklin Delano Roosevelt. He not only let the ABA and AMA talk him out of admitting Jewish refugees from Hitler—they didn't want competition from thousands of European-educated doctors and lawyers—but he made damn sure the cattle-cars kept rolling by refusing to bomb the rail lines going to the death camps as Jewish leaders begged him to."

"Who cares about history any more?" Albert snorted. "Most of our people don't even know that it was a Jew—Chaim Solomon—who made America possible, by raising hundreds of thousands of dollars for George Washington and the Continental Congress, mostly by meeting ships that came into port from every other country on the globe and convincing them—in their own languages, mind you—to invest in his new little country."

"Or that," Asher added, "unlike the general population of the thirteen colonies, a *majority* of Jews fought for independence." He sighed. "Sad to say, two thirds of America's Jews voted for the precise opposite of independence, George McGovern and Michael Dukakis. From 'Give me liberty or give me death!' and 'Don't tread on me!' to 'Where's the beef?' I'm terribly afraid that liberal Jewish support for this decade's brand of national socialism is planting the seeds for a virulent wave of anti-Semitism that'll make *kristallnacht* feel like a day at Disneyland."

The rabbi's guest nodded. "That's one reason I don't live here, Asher. Belgium isn't any better—in many ways it's worse—but it's where my business is. I wish there was a good political reason to set aside business considerations and live here, but there isn't, any more than there's a reason you should live in Belgium."

Outside, they heard a police siren wail as a squad car roared down the otherwise quiet residential street. It was a fairly frequent occurrence, Albert gathered, even in this rather nice neighborhood. Chicago was a city at war with itself. There were three sides, and only two—the freelance villains and those who carried badges—were allowed to own and carry weapons.

"Yes," Asher told him, "I see what you mean. I wondered why you don't live here. To me, *this* was the Promised Land after the war—it changed, almost imperceptibly, all around me: always more poverty, more squalor, more taxes, more regulations, more crime, all as the direct result of liberal policy-making—but I mean to see that it becomes the Promised Land again, someday."

"You and Simon Wiesenthal. A brave resolve. I salute you." Albert raised his snifter and drank. "I think this country's worst problems today arise from an equivalence that's been sold somehow between Judaism and socialism—you can't be a good Jew (or a good black, I've noticed) if you aren't also a good, politically correct, heel-clicking cluck—when in terms of Jewish moral philosophy and culture, nothing could possibly be further from the truth."

"You're right," Asher told him. "If they actually wanted to stop anti-Semitism, people like the ADL would encourage Jews to have guns. Anti-Semites are cowards; that would put an end to it. But they see anti-Semitism as a profit center, and they can't keep making money off it if it's over, can they?"

Albert rubbed the bridge of his nose between the eyes. "It must be very frustrating."

Asher grinned. "Indeed it is. I have a young friend, a novelist from California named Schulman, who asserts—and I believe him, Albert—that we Jews have been persecuted through the ages because for thousands of years each of us has spoken to God directly. Thus it was the Jews who invented individualism, and no king, bureaucrat, or dictator has ever forgiven us for it!"

"Excuse me, I don't think I see your point."

Asher spread his hands. "Only that some Jews unconsciously aspire, perhaps, to make up for our invention of individualism—and the wrath that it engenders—by espousing collectivism, statism, socialism, the Third Way, and all the rest of that failed bloody dreck."

"Oh, my ... " Albert was almost at a loss for words. "Dukakis and McGovern. What have we let ourselves become?"

"Groceries," Asher told him. "Groceries for monsters."

"What you're saying is that it could happen again," Albert suggested.

Asher replied, "Unless those of us who *have* learned something from history do something about it.".

CHAPTER TWENTY-TWO: ALLIE ZEDOWITZ

This time it was dark outside.

The bus trip to Ben-Gurion was more crowded than it had been on the way into Jerusalem. Although he'd have much preferred sitting in the back, John found himself directly behind the uniformed driver with a pleasant-looking young woman and her little girl, sitting on her lap, whom he estimated to be about nine years old.

He was interested to see that the driver, an overweight man with gray hair, wore a pistol in an open-topped holster with a strap. He wondered what it was, then realized with pleasant shock that a month ago he'd have been horrified to see the driver with a gun at all.

"Excuse me, Father, are you an American?"

John turned to the young woman. He'd momentarily forgotten that he was wearing clerical garb again. Whatever happened afterward, he'd decided, he would leave Israel as he'd come, as a Catholic priest.

"Yes," he replied. Her accent betrayed her as a westerner or midwesterner, a strawberry blonde with freckles and a light summer dress she'd regret as soon as she got back to the wintery States. "My name's John Greenwood. I'm from Chicago. And it's 'Monsignor'."

Her daughter was intently reading a paperback

labeled *Goosebumps* and didn't look up. The woman smiled. "It's good to hear an American accent again. Most people I know here speak English, but it's not the same; I never realized. My name's Allie Zedowitz, and this is Julie."

As freckled as her mother, the little girl looked up from her book and gave him a devastating smile. "We're gonna go ice skating!"

"Well that's two coincidences," John laughed. "My mother's name is Julia, and I'm a hockey coach. Where are you going to go skating?"

The mother put a hand on her daughter's shoulder. Then, as if she'd made a decision, told John, "In Colorado Springs. Neither of us has ever been there before—I'm from Omaha and Julie was born here in Israel—Colorado Springs is where my husband's mother lives, up around the Broadmoor on Mesa Drive."

"I see." Unconsciously, he'd shifted to father-confessor mode.

Allie shook her head. "Not entirely. Until recently, we lived in Tel Aviv where my Zack was a programmer. Two months ago we moved to a kibbutz. He'd always wanted that. He'd taught himself all about winemaking. But last week, while he was out in the vineyard tending grapes, happy as a lark, he was killed by a sniper's bullet."

"That must have been terrible. I'm very sorry." There was nothing he could say—short of magic words that would make it all go away—that felt adequate. But something had to be said, and he'd said it.

What surprised him was that Julie's nose was back in her book. He guessed she'd probably heard the story a thousand times by now. He wondered where she'd been when here father was killed. Did she see it? There was no telling how it would affect her later on in life.

"Thank you," Allie replied. "Julie and I are trying to be brave, that's what her daddy would have wanted. And I'm lucky I get along with my mother-in-law. We have friends, but no relatives here, so we're headed back Stateside to live with her, at least for a while."

"More coincidence," John was beginning to enjoy the conversation. "As I said, I coach for Catholic Youth Athletics, specializing in hockey. I've been to Colorado many times. Most recently Denver for a conference, but I've taken teams to Colorado Springs. They have quite a number of rinks for a city that size, at least six that I know of, including the famous World Arena Ice Hall, Sertich, and—"

Suddenly, something that was more than a noise rocked the bus and brought it to a violent halt. A flash strong enough to blind lit the night, but John had been turned away from it. When he turned back, he saw that the driver lay halfway out of the bus, draped over his broken steering wheel and the frame where the front windshield had been. The man's head was gone and the stump of his neck poured crimson out into the headlights of two cars that had stopped in front of the bus.

There was a lot of yelling outside, and then the shooting started.

A torrent of automatic gunfire poured into the bus, sounding like an old-time gangster movie. People screamed; John could hear bullets striking metal and glass all around him. The bus driver's body jerked each time it was hit. Not thinking at all, he seized Allie by one arm and pulled her down onto the steel floor with him, her daughter lying beside her. Both were strangely quiet, but the bus was filled from one end to the other with the noise of machinegun fire, prayers, and screaming.

Abruptly, John was aware of a pain in the back of his right thigh. It hurt worse than anything he'd ever felt before, even when, as a boy, he'd played a whole period with an arm he'd known was broken. So this, he thought in a detached way, was what it felt like to be shot.

Then he looked at Allie and realized, from the blood spreading across the left shoulder of her light dress, that she'd been shot, too. He didn't have any idea what to do for her, but realized the shooting had to stop or it would go on until they'd all been killed.

Crawling as quickly as he could—his leg really *hurt*; what idiot had told him bullet wounds don't hurt immediately?—he reached up, unsnapped the strap of the driver's holster, and pulled out the pistol. It didn't look exactly like his own gun—the name Browning was stamped into the slide—but it seemed to have the same controls. He cocked the hammer and only remembered at the last instant to check the chamber, which was unloaded. He worked the slide and felt a cartridge slip up into the barrel and the slide go into battery.

By that time the gunfire outside had let up, but the terror was far from over. A wrenching sound came from the back of the bus, and the big emergency door swung open. Four men climbed in, wearing Levis, running shoes, and the checkered headdresses he believed were favored by the Palestine Liberation Organization. They all carried AK47 machineguns.

As two of them strode forward over a dozen bodies lying in the aisle, the two at the back moved more deliberately. One aimed his weapon at the head of woman slumped in a rear seat and pulled the trigger, spraying blood and brains all over the window beside her.

John shot him.

Front sight centered in the notch of the rear sight, both sights level with each other, cloth-covered head sitting atop them like an apple on a post. Half-breath, squeeze-don't-jerk. He hadn't even thought about it consciously. Nor had he heard the gun go off or felt any recoil. All he felt was a mortal regret that he hadn't shot the criminal before he'd shot that poor, helpless woman.

What he knew now was that he must be fast if he wanted to live.

Swinging the pistol's muzzle, he shot the terrorist closest to him, coming up the aisle. The man stumbled and fell back with an inarticulately shouted curse and John shot the man immediately behind him who went down face-first, without a sound. He was preparing to shoot the fourth when he felt a hammer-blow to his chest. Apparently he hadn't killed the first man, who had a pistol out and aimed at him, its muzzle smoking in the headlights of the cars out front.

John shot him again, twice in the face. This time he heard the tinkle of spent nine millimeter cases on the steel floor of the bus.

The fourth man was behind a seat now, shooting at John. The bullets hit the dashboard of the bus, showering the back of John's neck with broken glass. It was hard for him to aim in the confusing light and shadows without hitting passengers. The terrorist saw that, and began to inch forward, using fallen bodies as shields.

John felt his strength begin to leave him.

He was certain most of the passengers on the bus had been killed or injured in the explosion or the first volley of gunfire. But in the seat immediately behind the one in which he, Allie, and Julie had been sitting, what now seemed like 10 years ago, he saw the heavily-veiled face of a Moslem woman as she reached out, trying to pull the little girl toward her, out of the line of fire. For some reason—although he knew it was irrational—the sight outraged him.

By now he realized he was mortally wounded. The fourth terrorist was advancing slowly. Bleeding heavily, John levelled the dead bus driver's pistol, aiming not at the head which hid itself behind the bodies of its victims, but at the complicated front end of the AK47.

He squeezed the trigger. The muzzle of the

assault rifle flipped back, striking the terrorist in the head. The man screamed curses—in English—and stood without thinking, bleeding, blind with fury. John shot him four times before his strength finally failed.

In the distance, he heard the *hee-haw-hee* of police cars coming. At the back of the bus, miles away, the first man John had shot crawled over several bodies and shouted "Let's get out of here!"

Somebody shouted something back and they were gone.

He wasn't aware that he'd laid down. He couldn't feel his legs, which was a blessing, he realized, because he recalled that he'd been shot in one of them. He saw a shadow hovering over him and forced himself to focus.

Allie.

Beside her were Julia and the Moslem woman.

"Father! Please, can you hear me? You saved our lives, Father!"

"Mom, it's 'Monsignor'." Tears streamed down the girl's face, and her mother was crying, too. "Hang on, Monsignor, hear the ambulance coming?"

He heard, but couldn't reply. He knew he had only moments left.

His last coherent thoughts were that two American Jews had been saved.

With a gun.

And that another Jewish baby wouldn't be taken in and raised by strangers to the faith, however kindly and charitable their intentions.

"Hitler has claimed too many!" he remembered Albert saying.

John slipped into unconsciousness, and death.

CHAPTER TWENTY-THREE: GABRIEL POSSENTI

The telephone rang.

Julia arose from the sofa where she'd been watching an old movie on television, and went into the hall to answer it. For perhaps the thousandth time in the last ten years, she thought she should get one of those wireless phones everybody else seemed to have. At one time it hadn't mattered, but she was lonely now and needed human contact more.

"Hello, Greenwood residence." These days she often expected it to be Ed calling from work, and then remembered, all over again, that he was gone.

"Mrs. Julia Greenwood?" The voice at the other end of the line sounded official. It had taken Julia over half a century of diligent work to suppress that very German reflex to fear and mindlessly obey such a voice—and replace it with a healthy American disrespect for authority.

"This is she," she replied evenly.

"Mrs. Greenwood, my name is Arthur V. Kittridge." His voice was smooth, comforting, but completely professional and removed. He might have been trying to sell her life insurance. "I'm a Junior Human Resources Liaison Officer with the United States Department of State. It's my most unfortunate duty to tell you that your son, Monsignor John Greenwood has been killed by

Arab terrorists in Israel."

There was a straight-backed chair in the hall-way beside the telephone stand. As far as Julia knew, no one had ever sat in it before. She reached out with a blind hand, found the chair, and sat down.

"Mrs. Greenwood?"

"I'm here," she told the voice. "Tell me, did he die without pain?"

"Your son died very heroically, Mrs. Greenwood. He was on a bus full of passengers that was attacked by terrorists on the way to the airport. The driver was killed instantly. Your son took his sidearm and killed three of the terrorists with it before they could shoot two dozen unarmed, help-less people, and he drove off at least three more. The Secretary of State is arranging now to give him a Presidential award."

"Posthumously." As if it mattered. She was tempted to ask why it was necessary for all those people to be unarmed and helpless, but he wouldn't have understood. Her husband had understood, and so had John before the end.

"Yes, Mrs. Greenwood, regrettably so. We'd like to fly you to the White House to accept it, if you would, directly from the hand of the President."

Julia thought about that for a long, long time. She wasn't so much concerned with a decision—that was easy—as with how to put it.

"Mrs. Greenwood?"

"Mister—I'm sorry, I don't remember your name."

236

"Kittridge, ma'am, Arthur V. Kittridge, Junior Human Resources Liaison Officer with the United States Department of State. The ceremony wouldn't be until next week. We'd send a limousine directly to your door, take you to O'Hare and put you on a special chartered flight. Then you'd take a helicopter from Dulles across the Potomac River, straight to the—"

"Stop, Mr. Kittridge, please." She felt her German accent coming back, as it did at times of stress. "I don't know whether you know it, but I've just recently lost my husband. He was murdered, too. Now you say that my son is dead. I have to tell you, Mr. Junior Human Resources Liaison Officer, that neither my husband nor my son would have approved if I accepted *anything* from the hand of the man you work for. I don't want you to bother me ever again, do you understand me?"

"But Mrs.—" In her mind she could see his hands flutter.

She frowned at the instrument. "Do you *understand* me?"

"Yes, ma'am, I do."

"Then good day." She hung up.

"Thank you for inviting me here," Sheila took a sip of the drink Kitch had given her and looked up at the man in surprise. Laphroaig, single malt. For a tweedy old professor, he remarkably good taste in whiskey. And this room was absolutely wonderful.

Then she regretted her evaluation of John's old friend. It had nothing to do with why she was here.

There was no one to impress. He was just being kind. And she had a lifetime of bad political habits to unlearn.

"You're welcome, Sheila." He took a sip of his own scotch. John had left his Nat Sherman's here; they were both smoking them in a kind of ceremony. The aroma reminded Kitch of the best friend he'd ever had. He noticed that Sheila French-inhaled as she smoked.

They were sitting up in the *camera obscura* because he wanted to remember John the way he'd seen him last. "I'm glad you were in when I called—and that John gave me the number. It appears I'm the last of his friends and family here in Chicago that he talked to, and I thought it was important that you and the others knew that he'd found something over there—I haven't a clue what it was—that gave him peace."

She nodded. "He was always such a troubled man, even in high school. Always concerned with doing the right thing—whatever that was. Always looking, never finding. Always doubting himself, when there was just no reason. He was probably the finest, kindest man I ever—"

Kitch exhaled raggedly, closer to tears than he'd been since childhood. "Me, too, Sheila. I hope he knew how much he meant to us."

Tears had begun to run down her cheeks, smearing her makeup. She leaned over and put her hand on top of his. "So do I, Kitch, so do I."

Not even aware that she had done it, Julia

pulled the silk scarf up over her head and entered the church. It was dark outside, and very cold. She hadn't brought her car into the city. The cab man had refused to wait for her and she didn't know how she was going to get home.

And this wasn't even her church, out in the suburbs, but his, the Church of St. Gabriel Possenti of Isola. Tomorrow she was supposed to come back here and claim his possessions. Eleanor, his secretary, had told her they were already packed up. Eleanor wanted her to come to lunch with her tomorrow at her own home. She thought maybe she'd do that; the woman, 10 or 15 years younger than herself, probably needed comforting.

Genuflecting and crossing herself, she approached the altar and reached for the taper to light candles for her dead son. Another hand got there first. She looked up. It was Father Joseph, John's young friend.

He smiled at her. Julia was amazed to see that he, too, had been crying. She smiled back and together they lit candles, knelt, and prayed.

In the Piper Arms, the old, comfortable hotel directly across the street from St. Gabriel's church, Albert Mendelsohn put the telephone down, reached up, and tore the lapel of his jacket according to Jewish tradition. Then he went to the closet-space, found his hat and overcoat, and left.

Downstairs, he had the captain get him a cab and gave directions to one of the city's older neighborhoods.

Throughout the long, cold cab ride, he kept asking himself the questions that had troubled him since the moment he'd heard John was dead. Had it been a *mitzvah*—a kindness, a good deed, a duty— to tell his nephew the truth about himself? Hadn't John died as a direct result? Or had it been something else—an *averah*, a bad deed, an exercise in vanity? Albert's grief made it hard for him to judge. Perhaps Rabbi Liebowitz could help him. He hoped so; he didn't think he could live long with what he was feeling.

At his destination, he got out, paid the cabby, and carefully walked up the freshly snow-covered sidewalk.

Asher met him at the door. Half a dozen other faces, eyes wide, expressive of concern and grief, greeted him, as well. Two were strangers—with Israeli accents. Together they went into the house and began saying the Kadish, the Mourner's prayer, for Asher's friend, Albert's nephew, Abram Herschel Rosen.

CHAPTER TWENTY-FOUR: THE PRESIDENT'S MAN

"Front and center!"

"Yes, sir!" both men answered simultaneously, fresh from their high velocity flight back from the middle east in a special pair of SR-71Bs the Outfit kept handy.

"Two massively-trained Special Agents wounded and three of our best local wetworkers dead. A fine impression to give our hosts on one of our first cooperative security operations! You let one damned little priest do this to you?"

The President's Man looked up from his desk at the two men staring down sheepishly at him. For an instant they looked at one another like schoolboys called to see the principal. One of them—the one named Galen if he recalled correctly—leaned before him on crutches, a huge messy handful of bandages covering one eye. It had taken several hours of surgery in Israel to repair the damage, but he'd see again.

The other—Fuhre—carried his right arm in a sling.

"One very large, *hockey-playing* priest with a Browning High Power!" Fuhre protested bitterly.

The President's Man was disgusted. What were things coming to these days? There'd been a time (under a different administration, to be sure) when an assignment like this would have been carried

241

out with discretion and dispatch. He'd done no little amount of it himself. He wasn't sure what had gone wrong over the years, but something sure as hell had.

He told them to sit down. They were in an office he was proud of. It was from here that the seige in Waco had been orchestrated and the final assault on Mount Carmel had been ordered. He'd been the one to order the site bulldozed and, two years later the site in Oklahoma City. It had been his idea to give medals to the men who had murdered Vicky Weaver while she was holding her baby. He often wondered what future archaeologists would make of all the evidence he'd buried.

For a moment, he contemplated having these two cretins eliminated. But the fact was that they'd done what they were told. That oldtime German style of ruthless, mindless obedience was an increasingly rarer commodity these days. The whole thing reminded him of a joke. A tourist had asked a farmer about his one-legged pig. "Why, that pig saved the lives of my whole family," the tourist had been told. "Woke us up and got us outside before the house burned down."

"Did he lose his leg in the fire?" the tourist asked.

"Hell, no—it's just that a pig like that, y'don't eat all at once!"

So he'd let Galen and Fuhre live.

For a while, anyway.

"Well," he said at last, you did accomplish your mission, and nobody suspects that it wasn't Arab

242

terrorists. 'Terrorism' is such a damned useful concept."

"I love it," Galen replied.

Fuhre sat silent.

"Okay then, here's the deal. You both get medals—the same one Lon Horiuchi got. You both get promotions. You both get raises. And you both get a new assignment in a different city, for a job well ... done, anyway."

Both men said, "Thank you sir!"

"Don't thank me, it's policy. Bishop Camelle, by the way, is hopping mad, but he'll get over it. He isn't the first man to say, 'Who will rid me of this meddlesome priest?' and then claim to dislike the result."

Both men chuckled although he doubted that they understood the reference.

"Now get the hell out of my sight!" He dismissed them with a wave of his stiff, out-stretched right arm. "And see if you can't do something about that damned irritating Jewish pro-gun outfit in Wisconsin!"

EPILOGUE

Gabriel Possenti was a Catholic seminarian who rescued the village of Isola, Italy from a band of 20 *banditti* in 1859 with a striking, one-shot, lizard-slaying demonstration of handgun marksmanship. He died in 1862 and was canonized by Pope Benedict XV in 1920. The Possenti Society promotes Possenti's Vatican designation as Patron Saint of pistol and revolver owners. It emphasizes the historical, philosophical and theological bases for the doctrine of legitimate self-defense.

The Roman Catholic church probably saved more Jewish lives during the Nazi reign of terror than any other institution. Pope Pius XII himself concealed refugees in his residence. Thousands of Jewish children were rescued and hidden by well-meaning Christians. Evidence suggests that some of them became priests and nuns.